The
PHANTOM
PIPER

D1387145

Also by Garry Kilworth

The Brontë Girls
Dark Hills, Hollow Clocks
The Drowners
The Raiders

for younger readers

Billy Pink's Private Detective Agency
The Gargoyle

First published in Great Britain 1994
by Methuen Children's Books Ltd
Published 1995 by Mammoth
an imprint of Reed International Books Limited
Michelin House, 81 Fulham Road, London SW3 6RB

Reprinted 1996, 1997

Copyright © 1994 Garry Kilworth

The right of Garry Kilworth to be identified as author of this
work has been asserted by him in accordance with
the Copyright, Designs and Patents Act 1988

ISBN 0 7497 2387 4

A CIP catalogue record for this title
is available from the British Library

Printed and bound in Great Britain
by Cox & Wyman Ltd, Reading, Berkshire

GARRY KILWORTH

The PHANTOM PIPER

Mammoth

This novel is for the late Elke Lacey, an exceptionally talented editor, who steered my novel, *The Drowners*, to a Carnegie Medal commendation, and whose advice was always offered with great care and sensitivity.

The Children of Canlish Glen

Sadie Burns 9 – shop assistant
Alistair Burns 12 – farm hand
Jenny McDonald 8 – piper
Jimmy Watson 12 – schoolmaster
Mary Watson 9 – general labourer
Heather Brown 7 – store owner
Robbie Mcleod 13 – baker
Alex Mcleod 6 – baker's assistant
Danny Mcleod 2 – baker's assistant
Angel MacPhearson 12 – church minister and farm hand
Morag Knowehead 13 – sweetshop owner
Hamish Cairns 10 – farmer
Elsbeth Cairns 11 – farmer

Contents

MEMORIAL PLAQUE

In 1552 an unusually mild winter in this region allowed unexpected access from the outside world to Canlish Glen. Encouraged by an English lord, rivalry between the clans was fierce at the time and territorial arguments raged between local chieftains. On 1 January of that year a massacre of the people of Canlish took place on the slopes beyond the high ridge.

In the early hours of New Year's Day a lone shepherd standing on the crags witnessed the impending attack of a clan hostile to the small village. The shepherd ran to his turf and stone croft, marked on the expanse of snow only by a lazy curl of peat smoke, and fetched his bagpipes. He roused the villagers from their beds with a martial pibroch.

Despite the shepherd's warning the entire adult population of Canlish was slaughtered on the snow-covered heather.

Chapter One

BAGPIPES IN THE DAWN

It was a freezing night in November. The harsh weather had come early and filled the glen between the mountains with snow. Sadic Burns woke to the faint sound of bagpipes in the hills. It was an eerie and mournful tune which she recognised as a pibroch: a difficult air to play which only skilful pipers attempt.

Still half-asleep, she sat up in bed and stared out of the window, into the murky dawn. She could see him, tall and straight, his glengarry streamers fluttering in the breeze, his bagpipes stark against the snow. The piper was walking high up, across the whitened crags, his swishing kilt disturbing the heavy mists. The martial dirge that he played seemed to move like a mist itself, rolling down the slopes of Ben Daw to the dark shapes of the houses below.

Sadie's tired eyes then beheld a sight which only partly registered in her fuzzy mind. There were people struggling up the slopes, up to the crags, whom she recognised. People from her own village. They seemed to be drawn to the tune, drawn to the piper, following him . . .

Sadie's eyes closed, the lids feeling heavy. Surely she was still dreaming? She fell back on the pillow once more. Soon she was fast asleep again, but with the piper's tune still playing in her head, growing softer and softer, until it was lost amongst the sound of wind-wailing hills and rushing burns of the Scottish Highlands.

When she woke again, she thought about the scene she had witnessed from her window, but decided it must *surely* have been a dream. Looking out now, over the snow, she could see nothing but white mist swirling round the crags.

This morning Sadie could not see the single meandering road running over the saddle between Ben Canlish and Ben Daw, hidden beneath the covering of white. A high, pretty village seeming to float on seas of alpine flowers and purple heathers in the summer, Canlish Glen was very often snowbound in the winter.

Sadie's brother Alistair came to her room.

'Mother's away out already,' he said. 'I expect she's gone to fetch the milk.'

Sadie was a little uneasy at this news, but still she said nothing, not wishing to appear silly. She washed and dressed and then joined her brother at the breakfast table. Alistair had warmed some tattie scones in the toaster and the children ate in silence. There was no fire in the grate, which was not like their mother. It was her first task in the mornings.

'It's the snow,' said Sadie, hopefully. 'It's making

her slow getting back from the farm. I'll call on the telephone, to see when she left there.'

Sadie liked using the phone. She picked it up and put it to her ear. Alistair saw a frown gradually appear on her forehead.

'It won't work,' Sadie said, looking disgustedly at the phone, before plonking it back on the cradle.

Alistair nodded. 'It'll be the ice,' he said, knowingly. 'Like last winter. You remember Mum moaned about it. When the ice builds up, gets too heavy, Mr Mcleod told her, and the weight breaks the lines.'

'Well, it's time they did something about it,' said the practical Sadie, her secret misgivings growing.

'Aye,' agreed Alistair. 'Anyway, we'll have to make our own way to school. You get your coat and scarf, Sadie, and don't forget your gloves. I'm going to wear my plimsoll shoes that were bought in Inverness.'

Sadie was shocked at her brother. 'Those are not for when there's snow on the ground! Your feet will get wet through. You need your boots, Alistair Burns. You'll get a skelping from our mother, so you will.'

Alistair scuffed the floor with his slippered foot, and said, 'Och,' knowing his younger sister was right, but desperate to wear his new black plimsolls, so that Robbie Mcleod would be jealous of him.

The children left the house well wrapped. Alistair had decided to wear his boots after all.

The snow was falling heavily as they walked to school. It was the kind of snow that crunched softly underfoot and stuck to the soles of the boots.

Around them the mountains were now clear and sharp, appearing like tall, sturdy sentries guarding the glen from harm.

Expecting to be late, the two children went straight to the classroom. There was only one classroom for all children up to the age of thirteen.

A riot was going on inside.

Alistair opened the door and was hit by a snowball. Jimmy Watson, the son of the school headmistress, had scooped the snow from a sill through an open window.

'Got you!' crowed Jimmy.

Jimmy still had on his pyjama top, which had been stuffed into a pair of trews. On his feet he wore slippers without socks. His sister Mary was wearing similarly mismatched clothes. Neither seemed to care about it.

There were paper pellets flying everywhere, pieces of chalk, wet blotting paper and aeroplanes made from sheets torn from work books. Alistair joined in for a while, shouting at Jimmy in a loud voice, and crying for assistance from his friend Robbie. It was only when things calmed down, after about half an hour, that Alistair realised no one was coming to start lessons.

'Where is everybody?' he said, parrying a blow from a ruler wielded by Hamish Cairns. 'Where's Mr Abarth? And where's your mother, Jimmy? Why aren't they here to teach us?'

Jimmy's face seemed to crumple a little.

'When we woke up, she wasn't there. Nobody was. All the grown-ups have gone.'

Alistair looked at Robbie and Morag, the two

oldest children in the class.

'Is this true?' he asked.

Morag said, 'It's true all right. Both my parents have gone somewhere. Robbie's the same. He came to call on me early and we looked all over. There's no one in the village over thirteen years old! It's my guess they've been called out on a search and rescue – for someone lost in the mountains.'

Alistair began to feel a little scared. His mother would never go out on a search and rescue. There was a team of men especially for that job: volunteers good at mountaineering. Why had *all* the adults gone?

'When are they coming back then?' he said. 'Doesn't anyone know?'

Robbie shook his head solemnly. 'They've just up and gone somewhere, awa over the mountains. We saw their footprints in the snow. Lots of them. They went up to the crags and then away over. I dinna ken where after that. I've tried phoning out, but I canna get the phone to work.'

'Well,' said Alistair, stunned by this information. 'Well.'

'Well what?' cried Morag, seeming more annoyed than upset. 'What are we supposed to do about it? That's what I'd like to know.'

Alistair bit his fingernail, then said, 'It's kind of spooky, don't you think?'

'You shut up!' shouted Robbie, suddenly flaring into open anger. 'You don't talk like that, you hear!'

Morag said quietly, 'Robbie's feared of supernatural things.'

11

'I am not!' shouted Robbie, confirming what she had said. 'I'm no feared of anything.'

'But it *is* spooky,' said Alistair, standing his ground against Robbie. 'It's never happened before, has it? It's as if they've been spirited away . . .'

It was then that little Sadie spoke.

'Alistair's right,' she said, in a quiet voice. 'It was me saw the grown-ups go. Just as the day was getting light. I thought I was dreaming, but I wasn't.'

This time Robbie didn't shout. He stared hard at Sadie, but he kept his mouth closed.

Alistair shivered and cried, 'Sadie, what did you see?'

Sadie struggled to remember exactly what she had witnessed, in the very early dawn, through the frost-crazed window of her bedroom.

'I thought it was a dream, because I was very sleepy, but there was a piper . . .'

'A piper?' cried Morag. 'Where?'

'There was a piper, up on the crags,' said Sadie. 'He was playing this tune – a pibroch, I think. He stood up on a high crag till all the grown-ups reached him, then he went off. He was still playing his bagpipes. They went with him.'

'You mean they followed the piper?' said Morag, swallowing hard.

'Followed him like sheep,' confirmed Sadie with a tight mouth. 'Followed the music he was making.'

Robbie said in a croaky voice, 'I've had enough of this – I'm going to light a fire.'

When he had gone, to fetch some kindling,

Morag said in husky tones, 'The Phantom Piper of Canlish Glen!'

Yes, they had heard the tale, of the piper killed in the clan wars many centuries ago, whose ghost was supposed to appear again one day to rouse the villagers from their beds and draw them up the slopes of Canlish and Daw. The shepherd piper had sworn an oath as he lay dying with a dirk in his breast. The people of Canlish would fight again! They would return to defend their village against impossible odds.

If Sadie's words were true, the piper *had* come again to call the clansmen and clanswomen from their beds, and lead them to their ancient battleground in the highlands.

'Angel MacPhearson,' said Alistair, turning to the minister's daughter. 'What do you say?'

Angel was the swot and if anyone knew anything, she did.

She nodded slowly. 'The anniversary of the battle of Canlish Glen,' she confirmed, 'will be on the day after Hogmanay, in six weeks time.'

Robbie returned to the room and threw the kindling down on the floor to attract attention.

'I don't believe in all this rubbish,' he snarled fiercely. 'An' I'll fight anyone who says it's true.'

No one cared to fight Robbie, not just because they were afraid of him and his hard fists, but because they didn't *want* it to be true. If their parents were out on a search and rescue, they would eventually come home, but if the piper had called them forth, then the children had been abandoned.

Alistair said, 'It's just a fairy tale.'

'Aye, just a fairy tale for bairns – there's no such thing as the piper,' Robbie snapped, and began to screw up some paper and stuff it in the grate, placing the kindling, stick by stick, on top.

The other children went back to their games, some went home for food, but then returned to the comfort of the group.

Later in the day, when the dusk was beginning to creep in, and the children were weary of playing noisy games, they gathered together around the fire. The enormity of the problem was finally beginning to sink in. Perhaps the adults really were not coming back? The children all sat in a circle in the middle of the classroom, some frightened, some miserable, some bewildered.

During the evening there were quarrels and disagreements over little things that normally wouldn't have mattered. Alistair knew that everyone was feeling betrayed and lost. Their parents had abandoned them, left them to the terrors of the night and the uncertainties of the day. Alistair felt as if he had fallen down a great pit in the earth and was now helpless against the nightmares that swallowed them all.

Robbie was still strongly adamant that the grown-ups would come back down from the mountain, but he agreed that if they did not appear before the next morning, something was seriously wrong, and that they should try to get help from outside.

'I think there's been a plane crash,' Robbie said, nodding emphatically. 'That's why they were all needed to go — my mam was a nurse before she married. They've all gone up there to help the victims.'

This sounded a reasonable explanation, though Alistair wasn't convinced. He was sure the adults would never leave the children *completely* alone. They would not all have gone willingly, especially some of the grandparents. Why, Angel's grandma was eighty-two years old! She wouldn't go up into the mountains in the winter, not for a dozen plane crashes. It didn't make sense. Still, Alistair did not feel inclined to argue with Robbie, not just yet.

'The first thing we have to do,' said Morag, 'is keep the fire going in here. We're all going to freeze otherwise. It's best we stay the night.'

'Aye. We'd better round up all the kids, especially the wee ains,' said Robbie. 'We'll keep them all here for now. Some of the bairns will be scared stiff. Let's have some volunteers, eh?' Robbie's dad had been in the Argyll and Sutherland Highlanders regiment, and Robbie fancied he knew the words to use and considered himself a right good organiser.

'Then tomorrow,' said Morag, 'Robbie and me will try to get help — we'll use the road over the twa Bens.'

'I don't think it should be you,' said Alistair. 'Someone else should go. The wee bairns will need someone older to look after them, especially Danny.'

Danny, Robbie's brother was two and the youngest child in the village.

'I'm no nursemaid, Alistair Burns,' snapped Morag. 'Someone else can look after the bairns.'

Elsbeth Cairns, Hamish's sister, said, 'I'll do that – I don't mind.'

Finally, it was settled that Robbie, Alistair and Morag would all trek up and over the pass, to reach the nearest town on the other side. They decided they would need provisions, in case it took longer than a day. They would need orange juice, bread and jam sandwiches '. . . and lots of chocolate,' said Alistair. 'We mustn't let our strength get low.'

They spent a fitful and restless night together, staring out of the windows, hoping for the sound of footsteps. Several insisted that the lights remain on, which made it difficult for others to sleep. There were sniffles from some of the children as the hours passed. Elsbeth Cairns and Sadie Burns cuddled up together, because they both suffered from bad dreams. Jimmy Watson's teeth chattered and he kept telling everyone he was cold, but most of them guessed he was scared.

No one came.

Alistair went outside once and stood under the stars to listen, thinking he could hear the adults returning over the pass. What he heard was the sound of the wind, screaming high up in the crags, carrying with it . . . what? Something – some inaudible sounds. The clamour of battle? The faint clatter of claymores clashing on tards? The war cries of clansmen sweeping down from the highlands, falling on their enemies in hand-to-hand fighting? The martial sound of drums, beating out a victory for the Donalds, or the Campbells, the Frazers or the McKenzies?

Perhaps his own mother was out there, a banner

in one hand and a dirk in the other, following the men into the fray, screaming Gaelic fury at the opposing clans, her wild red hair flowing about her tartan shawl, her sky-blue eyes burning with hatred? Alistair shuddered at the image. Yet, he had heard the tales from his grandfather, how his ancestors had fought against other clans, and the English, and the mountains didn't forget such terrible events, did they? The mountains were ageless and they kept their secrets alive.

'You're too imaginative for your own good, Alistair Burns,' he murmured, repeating something his mother had once said.

He went back inside, to the warmth and comfort, if not the security of his friends.

Heather Brown's parents owned the general store, and so she decided to open up her parents' shop. When morning arrived she provided the rescue team with all the necessary items, saying, 'Your mums and dads can pay for it later, when they come back again.'

The Mcleod brothers, Robbie, Alex and Danny, were the sons of the baker. Mr Mcleod had been in the middle of his baking when he was called away, for there was dough waiting to be put into the baking tins. The children all trooped through the bakery and scooped a handful of sticky dough to eat now. They were also given a hunk of bread by Robbie's brother Alex, for later in the day.

'If your dad's no back, and you have to bake the bread tomorrow,' said Angel MacPhearson, 'I'd be obliged, Alex Mcleod, if you would burn the crust nice and crisp an' black. Would you do that, Alex?'

'And for me,' chorused almost all the kids. 'I like it burnt nice and black.'

'Incinerated!' cried Angel, who knew a lot of good words.

'If my dad's no back, I will,' said Alex, gravely. 'I'll definitely sinerate it for you.'

Thus, armed with lemonade, bread and sweets, the trio set out for the pass.

In Alistair's heart, and he guessed the others felt the same, was a mixture of hope and fear. Fear because there was no logical reason for the parents' disappearance, and hope because if the three of them did get through to the outside world, they would have adults with them to help solve the mystery of that disappearance.

Chapter Two

WINTER LOCKS THE GATES

It was difficult to follow the road, because it was somewhere under the snow, but Robbie did the best he could. Morag kept her eyes on the gap between the Twa Bens, knowing that if they walked towards that spot, they would be bound to hit the pass at the right point.

Alistair found the going hard. The higher they climbed the deeper became the snow. Before long they were struggling in snow up to their armpits. What had looked so easy from down below became an impossible task. When they had started out, the sun had been slanting between the mountains, but now a swirling, sombre, grey sky was moving over. Alistair had lived in Canlish long enough to recognise a blizzard blowing in.

'We'll have to turn back,' he said to the other two. 'We canna get through this.'

Morag's lips were set in a thin line. 'We have to keep going,' she said. 'There aren't any adults down there, in our village. We'll be snowed in. How will we manage without grown-ups for a whole winter?'

Robbie, heaving for breath, nodded. 'Morag's right,' he said. 'We canna go back now.'

'Have you seen the sky?' said Alistair.

'Och, aye,' muttered Robbie, trying to wade through a drift, 'but what can we do? We've *got* to try.'

So they laboured on, with the season's white-wind weather crashing in around the ice-covered peaks of the mountains, its savage whirling skies threatening to descend and obliterate the three children. With their faces numb and their hands and feet agonisingly cold, they battled against the jagged edge of a day which came screaming down from the peaks, cutting into them with its saw of sharp ice. It was a day whose teeth broke into brittle fragments of ice, like tiny ceramic shards, and drove these sharp pieces into cheek and eye.

Their feet began to slip and slide on the frozen rocks beneath the snow. Robbie disappeared from view at one point and the other two had to drag him out of a filled crevice.

'We canna see what's under us,' whispered Alistair. 'We'll all be killed, falling into a deep chasm if we're not careful.'

'We have no choice,' said Morag, her previously determined voice faltering a little now. 'We have to go on.'

The wind began scything in from behind the high crags, its blade edge honed on the ice. Small hard flakes of snow came curving out of the now darkened skies as aerial rivers, sweeping across the slopes, covering black rocks which had once poked above the white mantle, changing the landscape. Soon there were no more landmarks, nothing to recognise. The glen and surrounding mountains had taken on a disguise, hiding their real identities beneath a huge sinister mask of white calico.

Robbie, Morag and Alistair struggled valiantly through the roaring wind and up the pass, as far as they could go, but were finally driven back by the blizzard. Drifts were piling up against even the smallest of rocks now, and the journey was becoming extremely hazardous. The cold cut into their bodies, the snow became deeper and more treacherous with every step, and there came a point when they had to turn back.

Even so, the return journey was hard. At one point the snow was so deep on the sides of the pass it reached the telephone wires on the top of the poles. Robbie wanted to look for the place where the wires had broken, so that he could try to join them, but Morag told him not to be so daft.

'Even if you find it, Robbie, what would you join them with? You can't just tie a knot and hope it works.'

Robbie was stubborn. 'Why is everyone always telling me what to do? How do you know I can't join them together? Maybe I learned it somewhere?'

'You did *not*, Robbie Mcleod, so stop showing off.'

They trudged on, their hands and feet like blocks, and their faces made of glass. They used the wrought-iron cross on the top of the sombre kirk, glittering with frosted icicles, as a beacon to guide them down the mountainside. It was visible in brief snatches, behind the chaotic turmoil of the blizzard, through occasional clear tunnels created by whirling gusts of wind.

The air became so cold that when Alistair licked around his mouth the spit froze painfully on his tender lips.

When the dark lanes of the dying light began to merge together on the glen floor, they finally reached the school again, and all three were exhausted.

Some of the children had been running around in the snow and had got wet. Angel had rounded them up and made them change their clothes. Jimmy Watson and Jenny McDonald had lit the fire in the main boiler and now the whole school was beginning to warm up, with hot water for the showers. Everyone gathered in a circle and Morag told them the worst.

'The pass is snowed up tight, kids,' she said, 'and we're stuck here. We have to make the best of it until our mums and dads, and aunts and uncles, and grandparents all come back again.

'It might be they'll come home tomorrow, or it might be that they'll no come home until . . . well, I don't know when. We have to decide what's best to do. Robbie?'

Robbie was still smarting over the telephone-line incident.

'Och, you do what you want, Morag Knowehead – why ask me? I don't know anything, do I? I'm just a dope.'

He turned his back on them and pretended to be more interested in a ruler than in their future.

Morag realised Robbie wanted to be persuaded to become involved again, but she was having none of it. If Robbie Mcleod wanted to play the prima donna, that was up to him. They had to get something sorted now, not next week.

'Well, how about you, Alistair – what do you think?' asked Morag.

All heads turned from Robbie to Alistair's direction. There were some bleak and frightened faces amongst them. It was really only just sinking in that the adults might not be coming back.

Robbie began rapping on a desk with the ruler, getting louder and louder, until Morag cried, 'Shut up Robbie – grow up, will you.'

'Grow up,' muttered Robbie, 'that's a good one.' But he stopped what he was doing.

Alistair guessed what the kids were all feeling, because it was inside him too. There was a dark terror there, a fear of all unknown things, against which the mere presence of adults normally protected them. But there were no adults. So those foggy shapes that moved through the mists of terrible dreams had to be battled by the children themselves, to be kept at bay with weapons like *common sense* and *reason*.

Alistair instinctively knew that there was a madness of a kind lurking in the shadows, waiting for them to let it loose amongst them.

'I – well – what we have to do is keep going as normal, right?' he said, his heart beating desperately fast. 'So we have to do the things the adults did. We have to – to keep everythin' going.'

Mary Watson said quietly, 'Do you mean we

23

have to do our parents' jobs, Alistair? Like Alex doing the bread and Heather opening the store? Not just for once, like we said, but every day?'

'Aye,' said Alistair. 'That's what we have to do. If we're to be here all winter, with no help from the outside, then we'll have to feed ourselves. Obviously we've no money to pay for things, so people will have to keep a tally of what's taken from the shops and from the farm. We'll need to mark it in exercise books — or something.'

'Where are we going to live?' asked Heather Brown. 'I mean, I don't want to live in my house all on my own. I get scared when it's dark. The windows go all black.'

Morag said, 'We'll all live here, at the school. There's toilets here, and we only need to keep one fire going.'

Hamish Cairns said, 'That's all right for you, Morag Knowehead, but you just have a sweetshop to look after. Up at the farm we've got the animals to care for. They've got to be fed, and the cows have got to be milked. Elsbeth and me can't come to the school to live. We can't keep going backwards and forwards like we did this morning.'

'That's true,' said Elsbeth, supporting her brother. 'We have to stay at the farm.'

Morag nodded. 'Well, there'll be some of us, like Alistair and Sadie, who have no jobs to do. Their mother is a weaver. Well, we don't need clothes, do we? We're not short of them, are we? What about Alistair and Sadie helping at the farm?'

'I don't mind,' said Alistair. 'What about you, Sadie?'

'I don't like the cows,' Sadie replied. 'And that dog, Black Gip, always tries to bite me.'

Elsbeth said, 'Och, it's 'cause you're feared of him, Sadie. You've no got to be feared of him.'

'Well, I am,' said Sadie defiantly, 'and I want to stay here, with Morag.'

'Fair enough,' Alistair said, 'but we need one more at the farm, at least. Any volunteers? What about you, Jimmy?'

Jimmy Watson stuck out his chin.

'I'm not doing any *work*, Alistair Burns, you can just take a running jump. I'm going to play all day, at whatever I please. for there's no one here to stop me.'

'That's an attitude,' said Angel McPhearson.

Heather Brown said shyly, 'I'll play games with you, Jimmy, if you want me to.'

'Well, I don't want you to, so there,' he said, cruelly. 'I don't like you.'

With this said Jimmy marched off to the corner of the room where he began sword fencing with an imaginary enemy. Undeterred by the rejection, which she was used to, Heather Brown went over and stood near to him while he jabbed and slashed at his foes. Jimmy ignored her.

Angel MacPhearson put up her hand.

'I'll come to the farm — if I'm allowed to ride Dinsie sometimes,' she said to the remaining children.

Dinsie was a blue roan, the pride of Elsbeth Cairns who had been given the pony for her last birthday.

'Dinsie is *my* pony,' cried Elsbeth.

25

'Well, I'm no coming unless I get to ride her,' replied Angel firmly.

Robbie swung round to rejoin the group and assumed joint leadership with Morag.

'Dinna fash yerselves,' grumbled Robbie. 'Elsbeth, you'll need to share your pony with Angel, just until the adults come back to the village, otherwise we'll be bletherin' till the thaw comes. Is that settled then?'

'I suppose so,' muttered Elsbeth, 'but she's still my pony, Angel MacPhearson, and you'll ride her when I say so.'

The first thing they did at the school was to fetch mattresses and bedding for everyone. Some, like Jenny McDonald, had sleeping bags, but most needed to bring sheets and blankets, and eiderdowns. It was not easy carrying heavy mattresses and bedding in the deep snow, but they eventually managed to get enough.

It was then suggested that they have a big snowball fight, before they dispersed to their various places of work. One or two of the older children saw that the wee bairns were well wrapped up, before they took them outside. The battle was a glorious one and the air was full of white missiles.

Mary Watson stood to the side, just watching, because she hated cold, wet hands. If a snowball landed near her, she glared and stamped her foot, but refused to move out of the way. When it was over, Alex Mcleod was in tears. He had been clouted behind the ear by a particularly hard snowball. Jeered at by his brother, he was comforted by Heather Brown, who promised him a slice of fruit cake.

By that time it was late afternoon and getting really dark. The cable which provided the village with electricity from the national grid, was an underground one and was still able to provide power. However, there were only one or two street lights in Canlish, which threw out a very poor jaundiced light upon a tight circle of snow. Heather Brown supplied most children with torches and batteries to comfort them while they were outside.

Provisions for an evening meal at the school also came from Heather's general store. Those who were staying at the farm, Alistair included, marched through the thick snow to the farmhouse. Alistair called in at his own house on the way, to collect his new plimsolls. If he could not wear them out in the snow, he could use them inside the farmhouse.

'Who's going to cook for us?' asked Alistair, once they were in the farm kitchen. 'Is it you, Elsbeth?'

'It is not,' said Elsbeth emphatically. 'We're all going to have to share the work.'

Angel said, 'We'll need to work a rota. Have you got pen and paper, Hamish? I'll work it out fair.'

'No need for that,' said Alistair. 'We'll just do turn and turn about.'

Their first meal consisted of opening two cans of baked beans and a tin of frankfurter sausages and heating them. They also fried some eggs. They would have had chips but they couldn't find enough fat to deep-fry them.

After the meal Elsbeth Cairns lit some hurricane lamps 'to save on the torch batteries' and then went outside to feed the stock. Hamish followed his sister and called for the other two to join them. They were so used to helping their parents with the livestock, they knew exactly what to feed them, and in which amounts, and at what periods of the day or night.

Elsbeth took Angel in hand and the girls put out the feed for the dozen dairy cows in the sheds. Then they raked and sluiced down the floor before laying fresh straw. After ensuring that the cows were warm and dry, they fed the domestic fowl, then hustled the chickens and ducks into their coops.

'If we leave any out, the foxes will get them,' said Elsbeth, 'and Hamish will want to use the shotgun.'

'Is he allowed to?' asked Angel, with wide eyes.

'No, but who's to stop him now?' said Elsbeth. 'He'll likely blow his foot off or somethin' daft. You know what boys are like when it comes to guns.'

Angel nodded sagely, as if she knew fine what boys were like, but not really knowing at all, since she had no brothers.

Finally the two girls went to feed the horses, the giant cart-horse with its hairy ankles and sturdy shoulders, and the more delicate Dinsie, whom both Angel and Elsbeth adored. Both animals got a fair share of stroking and petting.

Battling from barn to cowshed, from sty to stable, the children braved the stern discipline of the night, their lanterns swinging wildly in the wind. Black Gip, the farm's border collie, followed Hamish wherever he went, sometimes disappearing from sight under the deep snow. The cat wisely stayed indoors, watching with mild, disdainful interest through the frosted fern patterns on the windows of the kitchen.

Alistair found himself helping Hamish with the pigs, which he soon realised were quite frightening creatures when the big old sow charged at him, snorting and squealing, the moment he entered the sty to fill the trough. Hamish kept shouting, 'Don't let her get your ankle, Alistair, she gives a nasty bite. She's a wicked devil, Myrtle. She got my leg once and wouldn't let go, so stay out of her way.'

This piece of advice did nothing to bolster Alistair's courage, in fact it had the reverse effect, since it was impossible to keep one's footing on the icy uneven mud below the snow. Alistair became terrified of the big breeding sow and she would form part of his nightmares for many days and nights to come.

Finally, all the work was done, and the children went back indoors.

Alistair was relieved that it was all over for one day.

'You'll take the first shift, you and Alistair,' said Elsbeth to Hamish. 'We'll do the next one.'

Alistair said wearily, 'What's she bletherin' about, Hamish?'

'Milking the cows the morrow,' said Hamish matter-of-factly as he took off his coat. 'We'll be away up at five-thirty for that, so we'd best get some sleep.'

'Five-thirty?' cried Alistair, wondering what kind of hell he had got himself into. 'That's the middle of the night.'

'Och no,' said Hamish, seriously. 'It's just the

beginning of the day, Alistair. You'd no be able to sleep in any case, if we didna milk them. They'd be bellowing for us.'

For sleeping arrangements, they agreed that the two girls would use the parents' big double bed. The two boys declared they were used to having separate rooms and preferred to sleep alone.

In fact, once they were all in bed, the branch of a tree outside kept tapping on a window, and in the end Alistair went to Hamish's bedrom and lay on the floor beside his bed. Through the jumble of worrying thoughts and images came a mental picture of the piper standing high on the crags, calling his mother from her bed and leading her to a bloody battleground in the heart of nowhere.

Chapter Three

THE SECOND UNCOMMON DAY

In the middle of the night just after Alistair had gone to sleep, he was woken by a hand shaking him. Bleary-eyed he stared through the murk and saw Hamish's thin pale face floating before him. What was Hamish doing in his house? Then the high clear notes of a cockerel suddenly crowing in the yard below added to his confusion. Where was he?

Then he remembered and sat up quickly.

'Wha – what is it?' asked Alistair. 'Have the grown-ups come back?'

'Naw,' said Hamish, sullenly. 'It's time to get up. Five-thirty, remember? We have to milk the cows.'

Hamish had opened the window and there was an icy blast whistling through the room. The sound of the animals snuffling and shuffling in their stalls came from the sheds. Restless chickens were clucking in the coop. There were thick smells in the air, of damp straw and dung and silage. Strangely all this was a little comforting to Alistair, though he felt stiff and ached all over, from the long walk and the work.

'Five-thirty? But we just went to bed.'

'Naw,' said Hamish, in that disparaging tone again. 'We've had a good eight hours' rest.'

Alistair felt like flopping back on to the pillow, but he struggled to his feet and got dressed in the freezing draught from the window.

'Hamish,' he said, 'do we have to have that open?'

Hamish nodded, sagely. 'It's healthy, so it is. You have to blow away the cobwebs, Alistair. Come on, let's get the work done, then we can enjoy a good breakfast.'

Alistair followed Hamish down the stairs, grateful that he had not needed to wash in that cold room. In fact, he realised, there was no necessity for him to wash at all, ever. There was no one to check on him now. No one to tell him where he could or could not go. No one to make him do anything he didn't want to do.

He thought he should feel elated, but all he felt was immensely unhappy. He missed his mother dreadfully. There had been too much to do and think about yesterday, but he fully understood their plight. His mother was gone, perhaps never to return, and he and Sadie were to go on alone, without her. There was a hard knot of fear inside him which would not be easily undone.

Somehow it was an empty, cold, miserable world without the adults. You could probably have fun, when the work was done, but it felt a hollow kind of enjoyment. There was no one to tell him off if he did something wrong – even that seemed a necessary *part* of having fun somehow – but also there was no one to praise him when he did well at something. He felt like bursting into tears, but he held them back, biting his lip hard.

In the cold kitchen, Hamish stirred the ashes of the previous night's fire in the range. He then added some kindling to them. They soon flared into flame. After that he opened the flue, to get a draught of air blowing through, then placed some lumps of coal on the sticks, to start the fire afresh. Then he stood back, staring into the flames, and sighed heavily.

'What's the matter?' asked Alistair. 'The fire's going fine, isn't it?'

Hamish turned to face him and in the firelight Alistair could see his eyes were shining with tears.

'The fire's fine, but we're not, are we?' said Hamish. 'I mean, we can *try*, but will we get it right? What will my dad say, if he comes back and things aren't the way he wants them? He's an awful grouch when other folks don't get things right, Alistair. He likes things done his way. I really want my mam and dad back soon.'

Alistair put an arm around the younger boy's shoulders and was surprised to feel he was trembling.

'We all do, Hamish, and we'll get 'em back, you'll see.'

Hamish's face brightened a little.

'You really think we will?' said the ten-year-old.

'Of course we will,' said Alistair with more conviction than he felt. 'We'll get the kids together today and start right away.'

'Doing what?' asked Hamish.

'Well, that's what we've got to decide. Now, let's

get those cows milked, or we'll be here all day . . .'

Wrapped up well against the cold, their lanterns swaying, the two of them went to the cowshed and there Hamish showed Alistair how to milk the cows, using the brand-new milking machine. It was a strange business and at first Alistair was a little fussy about touching the teats on the cows' udders, but he soon got used to it. The first cow he tried gave out a terrible moan and shuffled her hooves when he tried to fit the milking machine to her teats. Alarmed he called to Hamish, 'This one's going mad on me!'

'Did you warm your hands first?' called Hamish.

No, he hadn't. 'Poor old girl,' said Alistair, stroking the cow's flank. 'Made you jump, did I?'

He warmed his hands under his armpits and tried again, and this time he was more successful.

When the boys had finished the chores outside, they went back to the kitchen. The girls had got up now and were cooking porridge on the range. It was warm in the kitchen and Alistair put his feet near to the range fire.

'You'll get chilblains like that,' Elsbeth warned him. 'You should get warm natural like.'

Alistair's feet were too cold for him to care. In fact he hoped they would drop off, so he wouldn't have to go through the awful pain of his blood circulating again. Black Gip came and licked his hand, as he was rubbing his feet, trying to get the feeling back into them. There were some things Alistair liked about being a farmer, and having a dog was one of them.

He had never had a pet, the cottage being too

small, or so his mother had always told him. Now there was a dog *and* a cat. He liked the musty odour of Black Gip's greasy coat, and soft feel of the cat's fur. He liked their mysterious ways.

And these were not Alistair's only pets on the farm. Outside, were a dozen or so other animals to care for. Then he suddenly remembered the great old sow and his blood ran cold. Some of them, he decided, he could do without.

Over breakfast the girls, too, admitted they were feeling miserable without their parents.

'It's no as if we ken when they'll be back,' said Elsbeth.

Angel nodded. 'But they *will* be back. We have to believe that, or we'll not get through the winter.'

Robbie Mcleod and Morag Knowehead arrived. Kicking the snow off their boots, they came into the kitchen and sat at the table, grateful for the tea they were given. Alistair told them about what the farm children had been discussing and Morag nodded.

'We've been talking about the same thing, haven't we, Robbie? The bairns are missing their mams and dads, especially wee Danny, so they have to see us bigger kids trying to get them back.'

'How do we do that?' asked Alistair. 'I don't understand.'

It was Robbie who explained it to them. 'You know I don't like this stuff about the Phantom Piper, but Morag says it's all we've got – well, to get the grown-ups back again, so it's got to be the piper . . .'

He paused for breath, and continued. 'The legend says the piper has called the grown-ups forth to defend the village from its enemies, back in 1552. There's only one way we can get them home to our time – we have to play the same tune as the piper played, standing on the crags.

'Now,' he said, seriously, 'there's only one person who can play the bagpipes at all, and that's wee Jenny McDonald.'

'She's such a *shy* lass,' said Elsbeth.

'Aye, but she's aye good on the pipes,' said Robbie. 'At least, she *could* be, with a bit of practice,' he amended, hastily. 'Jenny's got a lot o' puff for her age. She's been blawin' up a storm at the school. Did you no hear her this morning?'

'No,' said Angel. 'It's probably the snow, muffling the sound. If she stood on the crags, we would, nay bother.'

'Well, the crags are too dangerous at the minute, but when we know the tune, we'll take her up there,' said Morag. 'In the meantime, we've got to get Jenny practising pibrochs and such, until she can play one right through to the end. We've got to build up her wind.'

Alistair said quietly, 'You soon changed sides, Robbie – yesterday you laughed at the piper story.'

Robbie glowered at Alistair. 'I'm no so sure going up on the crags is a good idea. So far as I'm concerned it's looking for the pibroch that's important. Anyway, I'm entitled to change my mind if I so wish, Alistair Burns, and if you're looking for a punch on the nose, I'll give you one.'

'So that's the answer, is it?' said Alistair. 'Punch somebody and it'll make everythin' all right?'

Robbie bunched his fists, but after a few

moments uncurled them again.

'Come outside, you two,' he said, pointing to Alistair and Morag. With that he marched back out into the snow. Morag shrugged at Alistair and followed him. Alistair wasn't sure what was going to happen, but in the end he too went out.

Robbie stared at the ground while he spoke.
'Look, you two, I'm not right set on this idea of the piper – not by a long chalk – but I canna just sit and do nothing. The bairns and such have got to have something to believe in, so I'm going along with it, just for now, because there's nothing else to do. I want my mum and dad back, so I do. I'll go along with it, but . . .' he looked up fiercely, 'you two stop getting at me for everything, see? I can't seem to do anything right by you. Just stop picking.'

'All right,' murmured Morag.

'Sorry,' said Alistair, quietly. 'We've got to keep our heads, that's all.'

'That's why I'm agreeing with you,' replied Robbie, 'about this piper thing.'

'You're not agreeing with *me*,' said Alistair. 'I'm no right dead set on it myself – though Sadie says she saw the adults walking up over the pass . . .'

'Following the piper,' Morag said.

' . . . aye, following the piper. And I've never known Sadie to tell that kind of untruth before. She doesn't make up stories to get attention. So what I'm saying is, there must be *something* in it.'

The three of them shook hands gravely and went back inside to Hamish, Angel and Elsbeth.

Hamish was still worried.

'Do you mean no one knows the piper's tune?'

37

'Not yet,' said Morag, 'but Sadie heard the piper and we've got to get her to remember it.'

'Sadie?' exploded Alistair in heavy disappointment. 'She's got a memory like a sieve. She can't remember her own name sometimes.'

Though Alistair was very fond of his sister he was aware of her shortcomings, and as a brother he naturally expanded those shortcomings into greater failings than they actually were.

Morag said, 'Be that as it may, she's the only one who heard the piper's tune. It was a pibroch, she ken's that much. What we'll do is play some records to her. If that disna work, then we'll get all the sheet music in Canlish and go through it. And if that fails too, then we'll all sit round humming pibrochs till they drive us barmy. Somehow, sometime soon we'll find the tune played by the Phantom Piper of Canlish Glen.'

'Jings and crivvens, help ma bob,' cried Robbie, copying his father, whose favourite cartoon-strip character was a boy named Oor Wullie, famed for such expressions.

They all went outside to watch Elsbeth and Angel take turns in riding Dinsie. The pony was quite frisky in the cold morning air, but both girls knew how to handle her. While this was going on, Robbie and Alistair went for a walk amongst the pine woods at the back of the village.

'We could hunt while the adults are gone,' said Robbie, 'for deer and such.' He pretended to aim a gun and shoot something running through the trees.

'Aye, we could,' replied Alistair. 'An' for wildcats too.'

'Things to eat though — mountain hares and such.'

'Aye . . .' Alistair answered, then he stopped dead still in the silence of the trees.

Robbie looked at him quickly. 'What? What is it?'

'Can — can you no hear that sound, Robbie?' Alistair looked up, at the cliff face behind trees which climbed upwards to the rugged peaks of the mountains at the back of the glen. 'Are you sure you canna hear it?'

'What?' asked Robbie, looking frightened.

Alistair shook his head. 'I don't know — men shouting? I think — I think I hear the pipes too. Is Jenny practising?'

'She said her lips were sore — she's been blawin' all morning.'

'What if they're all around us, Robbie?' whispered Alistair, still staring at the mountains. 'What if they're fighting with the clans at this very minute — fighting and getting killed.'

'What are you bletherin' about, Alistair,' cried Robbie. 'You're scaring the breeks off me.'

Alistair shook his head. 'Nothing,' he said, turning back towards the farmhouse. 'Maybe it's just the wind. But I just thought of something else.'

'What? What did you think of?'

Alistair turned and stared his friend in the face.

'If we're going with the piper legend, then we have to get the adults back before Hogmanay.'

Robbie's eyes looked hollow with lack of sleep.

'Why? Why do we?'

'Because,' said Alistair, 'all the adults in the village were slaughtered the day after Hogmanay.'

Chapter Four

THE LONELINESS OF ALISTAIR

Alistair and the other farm kids went back with Morag and Robbie to the schoolhouse. The weather was foul. Great clouds were rolling into the valley to create a thick mist. A strong wind was still blowing in through the Twa Bens, bringing with it the loose snow from the mountain slopes, and swirling it along the streets.

Once in the schoolhouse the children began to discuss the future. Morag said she realised everyone was missing their parents but she was sure they would be able to get the adults back again soon. 'In the meantime,' she announced, 'we have to make sure that we don't run wild. I don't mean we've got to be angels, but just because there's no adults to tell us off, doesn't mean we can do as we like, any of us.'

Jimmy Watson said, 'Och, don't be an auld spoilsport, Morag Knowehead. It's our chance to break the rules without getting told off by some grown-up.'

'That's exactly what I'm talking about,' said Morag, seriously. 'We have to make sure we keep to the rules as best we can. The time to break them is when the adults are here, not when they've gone.'

There were many in the room who thought Morag Knowehead a prissy-missy after this statement.

'If there's going to be no grown-ups, we might as well have a good time playing games,' grumbled Jimmy Watson. 'Fighting games, and such.'

'*You* can play fighting games, Jimmy, but without the grown-ups it'll get too wild. It'll get out of hand. Don't come running to *us* when Robbie Mcleod bashes you too hard. That's right, isn't it, girls?'

There was a total silence from the other girls, but whether it was because they were too shy to speak up, or whether they agreed with Jimmy, was impossible to tell. They simply kept their peace.

Robbie stood up. Jimmy looked smug as Robbie opened his mouth to speak, certain that the rough boy of Canlish Glen would be all for breaking the rules. Certain that cissy girls like Morag Knowehead would be put in their place.

'Listen,' said Robbie seriously. 'I agree with Morag. Anyone who goes breaking the rules has me to deal with.'

He sat down again. Jimmy was aghast at what he saw as a treacherous turn-round in ethics.

'Who said you could act like a grown-up, Robbie Mcleod? You don't tell me what to do. My father does that,' said Jimmy.

Robbie said, 'Your father's no here, is he, dope?

Since he's no here, then I'm in charge – me an' Morag. If we say you'll stick to the rules, you will so, or I'll knock your block off, Jimmy Watson.'

'You can't talk to me like that . . .'

'I just did,' said Robbie, 'an' any more of your lip, Jimmy, and I'll thicken it for you.'

'Well, what *are* the rules?' cried Heather Brown, as Jimmy went into the sulks.

Morag replied to this. 'You ken fine what the rules are, Heather. You ken what's right and wrong, and all I'm saying is, if we don't act normal, then we'll get into trouble amongst ourselves. We have to all agree on this. Let's vote.'

So a show of hands was given, and the verdict was a majority vote in favour of keeping to the rules.

'That's good,' said Morag. 'I'm glad. We don't want anything terrible to happen in Canlish, do we? We want the adults to come back and see what a good job we've made, looking after ourselves, and when they do that they'll give us credit.'

'If we're doing our parents' jobs,' said Jimmy Watson, jumping up, 'that means I get to be schoolteacher. You all have to do as I say, when we're at lessons.'

There was a general groan throughout the whole group.

Heather Brown said, 'Do we have to?'

Morag nodded her head sagely.

'We have to do *some* lessons,' she said. 'We don't know how long the adults will be gone.'

There was another, less audible groan.

Jimmy Watson cried, 'Right, I'll tell you all what

to do. There'll be four hours of lessons a day . . .'

'Let's not go mad,' growled Robbie, who was not sure he was on Morag's side in this one. 'Some of us have got to work too – at the bakery and such.'

'That's true,' said Morag. 'Lessons will be two hours a day, from ten o'clock to twelve, with no breaks, so we get them over with in one go. Jimmy obviously can't *teach* us, because he doesn't know enough, but he's responsible for setting the lessons, like geography on Thursdays, that sort of thing. We'll have to learn from our books, and the older children can teach the younger ones. We'll muddle along as best we can, but we have to do *something*, or we'll grow up ignorant.'

'I'm beginning to think,' grumbled Hamish Cairns, 'that the piper missed one of the grownups.'

Morag put her hands on her hips. 'Meaning me, I suppose?'

'Aye,' said one of the smaller children. 'You're too bossy by half, Morag Knowehead.'

Alistair wanted to speak now.

If someone had asked him *before* the adults left, what he would do when they were gone, he would have told them without hesitation that he was going to have a holiday. He would have said he was going to have fun, enjoy himself, laze about and play games.

Now it had happened, however, he felt again that their going away had let something else into the glen. It was as if some nightmarish thing had arrived, ready to fill the empty space left by the adults. He didn't know what it was, and he couldn't

43

describe the feeling to anyone else. It was shapeless and evil and just waiting to be asked to come in. He just knew this *presence* had to be kept at bay. It was, he had to admit, very frightening. He didn't know *exactly* what he was scared of – something too foggy to put into words – but there was a darkness waiting to move into their village, dangerous and harmful, which only normal, everyday behaviour would keep out.

'We have to do as Morag says,' Alistair confirmed, 'or something terrible might happen.'

'*Something terrible will happen*,' mimicked Alex Mcleod.

Everyone laughed at this, but it was a strained laughter. No one actually challenged him outright.

Morag continued once she had quiet again.

'Angel will run the service for us on Sunday, at the kirk, same as her father did.'

Angel said, 'There's some things I can't do.'

'Well, we'll just miss them out, is all,' said Morag, 'but we'll have prayers and hymns just the same.'

After the meeting broke up, those children whose parents had stores and shops, went to open them up. Morag opened the sweetshop.

Heather Brown placed herself behind the counter in the Canlish General Stores.

Robbie and his two brothers went to the bakery. They could often be seen, their arms flour-white up to the elbows, kneading dough or taking freshly baked loaves from the ovens. The bakery became a meeting place, a collecting point, for the smaller children, who liked the smell and the warmth to be

44

found there of an early frosty morning.

The rest of the day was spent in trying to help Sadie Burns remember the tune the piper played. However, though they went through a dozen or more records of bagpipe music, lots of sheet music, they could not get her to agree on any of the pibrochs.

'It's no use,' she told them, 'I'm trying my best, but I canna remember the tune.'

Jenny in the meantime practised her playing.

'That's awful!' yelled Jimmy Watson. 'It sounds like two wildcats fighting.'

Jenny let the mouthpiece fall from her lips and said, 'You canna even *play* a note, Jimmy Watson.'

'Wouldn't want to,' crowed Jimmy, jumping from a desk top to the floor. 'Couldn't care less.'

'It's up to me,' said Jenny, 'to get the grown-ups to come back again.'

'Don't want 'em back,' sang Jimmy. 'Couldn't care less.'

Jenny made a face and went back to playing a tortured version of 'The Skye Boat Song', followed by 'The Blue Bells of Scotland'.

'They're easy,' shouted Jimmy. 'I can whistle them better than you can play 'em.'

But Jenny let the pipes drown the dissenter's voice.

By the time the evening came round again, all too early in the winter time, they were still no nearer to discovering the piper's melody. The farm children went back to the farm, to do their various chores amongst the domestic stock, and the rest of them settled down for the night in the schoolhouse. Little

Danny Mcleod was crying again, but Mary Watson comforted him, rocking him off to sleep.

'At least we're warm and well fed,' said Morag, 'but I wish the wireless would work proper.'

When they turned it on, the voices and music were drowned by the crackling created by the high storms.

At the farm there was a lot of work to do, which would have been a source of complaint, except that every one of the children involved knew there was no one else to do it. There was something special about being necessary. They all felt it, not just the real farm children – Elsbeth and Hamish – but Angel and Alistair too. They felt important, and indeed they were, to the whole scheme of things. Without them, the animals would die, and such a terrible thought kept Alistair going, though he was weary to his bones.

That evening, they all sat round the fireside, gazing into the flames, drinking cups of cocoa. Angel stared at Alistair across the small space between them, and smiled at him. She showed him her hands, the skin of which had suffered under the day's work. It was clear that normally her nails were kept neatly trimmed and clean, and that she was proud of her slim, delicate fingers.

It was then that Alistair noticed, for the very first time, how blue Angel's eyes were. It made his blood race like a burn gone barmy, just to look into those eyes. It was true she still had old-fashioned plaits, and a few small spots on her chin, but all the same Angel was nice-looking. It was a pity he secretly owed his heart to Morag Knowehead.

'Aye,' he mumbled, suddenly embarrassed. 'Your hands are a wee bit scratched. That's a shame.'

'Well,' sighed Angel. 'I don't expect it matters. They'll be a lot worse before the grown-ups come home.'

'Aye, I expect they will.'

'And I'm getting to ride Dinsie, aren't I?'

'You are that, Angel, and very good at it you are too,' said Alistair, seriously.

He was rewarded with a sparkling smile.

The children went to bed early, each one of them feeling the exhaustion that hard physical work brings. It seemed strange to Alistair that now they could stay up as late as they liked, it was fatigue that forced them to bed. Morag had warned them of the dangers of breaking the rules. Alistair was so thankful to get some rest he almost fell up the stairs.

In the middle of the night Alistair woke with unnamed terror. The sweat was pouring from his brow, soaking his hair and the pillow beneath, and he sat up with a jerk. For a while he stared into the impenetrable darkness, listening hard, and, when a fox gave out a cry like a bird in pain, he almost shouted for his mother.

Remembering that if he did call, no one would come except other frightened children, he kept quiet. It was an awful feeling, knowing that there were no adults out there, anywhere, to save him from the horrors of the night.

After a while he realised he was much too terrified to go back to sleep, in case he should continue with the same dream, or rather, nightmare. He could not remember what it was, but he knew it was a bad one. There was no comfort either, in lying awake staring into blackness. He decided he could not remain in bed, in *that* bed, for a moment longer.

Alistair felt he could not go into Hamish's bedroom for a second night running. So he crept out of his own room and went downstairs, where Black Gip was sleeping by the remains of the fire. The dog lifted his head and stared as Alistair came into the kitchen.

'It's only me,' whispered Alistair, wondering if the dog would recognise him in his pyjamas. 'Dinna worry.'

Black Gip's head lay back down, as if he understood exactly what had been said. His eyes remained open, but soulful, not in any way concerned by Alistair's movements. He simply watched.

Alistair poked the fire, trying to get the flames to start up again, but was unsuccessful. Then he went to the window and stared out into the night. Suddenly he began to feel angry at his mother for leaving him and Sadie. She should not have allowed herself to be caught up in something that made her abandon her children. She should have been prepared for such a thing and thwarted it.

'You shouldn't have gone,' he said furiously, under his breath, hot tears stinging his eyes. 'You left us here alone.'

Then he realised, hopelessly, that adults *never* really believed in supernatural things. They couldn't let themselves believe in magic, so they could hardly make arrangements to deal with strange events when they did happen along. They simply shut their minds off from such things and smiled when children said something scary was going on.

The night outside was surprisingly gentle in its aspect, with a soft silver light resting on the snow.

The darkness in his bedroom had been the result of the heavy curtains up at the window, rather than the night itself. In fact the stars were out and they sparkled as they always had done. A slim shaving of moon shone above the barn, casting its own light upon the outbuildings and snow.

Wherever she is, thought Alistair, my mum can see that same moon.

The thought brought her closer to him, made him feel less isolated and alone. He wondered if all the kids felt the way he did: deserted and lost. Perhaps they were all afraid, just like him, even Robbie Mcleod. Alistair hadn't shown how scared he was, so why should they? Only wee Danny had cried openly, in front of everyone, but then he was just a bairn.

This didn't mean that everyone was feeling strong though. Alistair would like to bet that half of them had cried into their pillows that night, now that the awful truth had sunk in. *The adults weren't coming home again – not until the tune was found.*

On a whim, Alistair put on his boots and coat and went out the back door, to the cowshed. There was a marvellous peace in the stalls, even with the shuffling of the animals and their occasional grunting and creaking. He remembered that Jesus had been born in such a place.

Alistair sat on a milking stool for a while,

listening to the cows, smelling the strong odours. After a while he went to one of the empty stalls and lay on a pile of newly strewn straw, and fell fast asleep.

When he woke, shivering with the cold, the grey light of dawn was visible through the cracks in the cowshed walls. Alistair got to his feet and was surprised how fresh he felt. He knew it was still very early and he should be drooping the way he always did at that hour.

By the time Hamish entered the cowshed, Alistair was halfway through the milking.

'I wondered where you were,' said Hamish. 'I looked everywhere.'

'Sorry,' said Alistair. 'I woke up so I came down here. I've started the milking.'

'Nearly finished, you mean,' said Hamish, sounding almost piqued that he had not been needed.

'Aye, I'm sorry I didn't wait for you, but I thought you were still abed.'

'Och, it's all right, I suppose,' replied Hamish with a grin. 'Come on. Let's finish up and get some breakfast. I'm starved.'

'Me too,' said Alistair.

Chapter Five

A DISCOVERY IN THE SNOW

Jimmy and Mary Watson were – a rare thing for a brother and sister of their ages – very close to one another. They seldom fought, they were considerate to one another, and they never needed other children to enhance their play. It wasn't that they didn't enjoy being with others, they did very much, but they didn't *need* them, because they were never bored.

There was one exception to this not needing anyone but themselves and it only applied to Jimmy. The exception was Morag Knowehead, the cool beauty of Canlish Glen. Jimmy, like all the other boys in the village, was soft on Morag. Intelligent, with classic features, Morag ruled the hearts of all males over the age of ten. Since the adults had gone though, Morag seemed to spend all her time with Robbie Mcleod and Alistair Burns, and hardly noticed the outwardly blithe Jimmy Watson at all.

Jimmy tried his best to attract Morag's attention.

He painstakingly planned the lesson periods, producing a chart of what should be studied by whom and at what times. He sounded the school bell at the beginning of lessons, ushered the children into the classroom, handed out pencils and notebooks, helped find textbooks when they were required, all that sort of thing.

Morag told him he was doing a good job, but there was no affection in her tone. When she was with Robbie or Alistair she sparkled, but when they were not around, she seemed serious. Jimmy wanted her to sparkle when she was with *him*.

What was really irking Jimmy was the fact that Robbie Mcleod seemed to have declared himself the overall leader. He seemed to have naturally assumed the position. Jimmy was sure it was for this reason that Robbie was receiving a lot of attention from Morag. Jimmy was only a year younger than Robbie, and thought himself a lot brighter, so he asked himself why *he* shouldn't be the leader? Why Robbie Mcleod? Why not Jimmy Watson?

Of course, Jimmy would say nothing to Robbie about it, but he tried to get Alistair on his side.

'We could lead the kids as well as Robbie,' he told Alistair with a smile. 'Why don't you tell him we want to be leaders for a while, eh, Alistair?'

'*You* tell him,' Alistair had said. 'I don't want to be leader and anyway, I'm not looking for a punch on the snoot.'

So, despite his outwardly cheery disposition, Jimmy was dissatisfied with the situation. The result was that early one morning he and Mary got together and decided to try to do something about it. Jimmy felt that if he could show Morag he was a hero, she would drop Robbie Mcleod like a hot coal and become *his*, Jimmy's girlfriend, instead.

'Mary,' said Jimmy, 'Sadie Burns is *never* going to remember that pipe tune, and we'll be stuck here with Robbie Mcleod lording it over us until spring.'

'I think you're right,' said Mary, 'but what can we do, Jimmy?'

'Look,' said her brother, 'I know Robbie, Alistair and Morag tried to get over the pass, but perhaps the day they went was a very bad one. Maybe if we tried – you and me – maybe we could do it, and fetch help from the outside.'

'D'you think so, Jimmy?' she said, sweetly. 'It looks awfy snowy out there.'

'Aye, it is, but we can do it, I'm sure we can, Mary.'

So without further argument, the pair of them got dressed up in the warmest clothes they could find, and slipped off without anyone else seeing them. They trudged through the snow at the back of the town, towards the pass. Even before they got out of the houses they were finding the going hard.

The sky that morning was full of cirrus clouds like lazy paintbrush strokes across the sky. In those brush strokes was a warning of foul weather to come. Jimmy kept looking up at the streaked heavens as they struggled on, knowing that if they did not make it over the pass between the Twa Bens and on to the next town, which was by no means just over the ridge, they would be caught in a storm and perhaps freeze to death.

'Are you all right, Mary?' he asked, for the twentieth time, as they battled on.

Mary's breath was coming out in whistles, but she nodded her head, not willing to give up just yet.

Before they were even a few metres up the wall of the glen, they were up to their necks in snow. Jimmy knew it was hopeless and so did Mary. Jimmy turned and looked at the village below them. Smoke was drifting upwards from the schoolhouse chimney and it was the only building, apart from the farm which they could not see, whose dark slate roof was visible through the snow.

The sound of the pipes came up from the schoolhouse. Jenny was practising again. The afternoon before they had found some old sheet music in a trunk in Heather Brown's house. Angel MacPhearson had been fetched from the farm. Though Angel couldn't play the bagpipes, she could read music. She had hummed some of the tunes to Jenny, saying incomprehensible things like, 'Of course it's in bass clef on the sheet, but I'm humming it in treble clef.'

'Of course,' Jenny had replied, not understanding a word because she played by ear.

Jenny was now dutifully playing some of these tunes, no doubt with Sadie in attendance.

'That noise is driving me crazy,' grumbled Jimmy. 'Don't they know it's useless?'

'Och, never mind,' said Mary, taking his hand. 'We're trying, that's the important thing.'

Jimmy sighed and looked around him at the snow-locked hills and rugged white peaks. 'And we didn't even get as far as Robbie, Morag and Alistair.'

'No, I don't expect we did, but then the snow wasn't as deep at the beginning.'

Jimmy nodded, still feeling disappointed. 'We didn't even get as far as the plaque.' His eyes strained against the whiteness of the snow and ice. There was a sharpness about the air today which, contrarily, made the scene difficult to look at. It was *so* clear that it made his eyes water and as he stared the shapes of the landscape seemed to dissolve and reform with different contours. He shook his head and was about to head back for the schoolhouse, when Mary gave a little cry.

'What is it?' he said. 'Are you all right, Mary?'

'I'm fine,' she said. 'But look just up there, on the side of the glen! It looks like something.'

Jimmy stared in the direction in which his sister was pointing and for a few moments thought he saw an ancient Highlander standing there, in full battledress – kilt, dirk, bonnet, claymore and tard. The man had a huge black beard above which were two piercing eyes and below which was a bunch of lace at his chin. The image was shimmering in the crystal air.

Jimmy blinked and the shape dissolved into a rock with white patches in its crevices.

'It's – it's just a stone,' Jimmy gasped.

'No, not *that*,' said Mary with some impatience. 'There's two bundles underneath it.'

Jimmy stared and saw what she meant.

'Let's go and look,' he cried.

When they reached the bundles they saw that

they were two bodies clothed in rags, draped around a crag, where the snow was shallow. They were not moving, either of them, and were perhaps dead from the cold on the mountainside.

'Is it two of the parents?' asked Mary, horrified.

'Why would it just be the two of them? When they come back, it'll all be together, as the legend says. I think it's probably two rescuers, got stuck there overnight. That's what I think it is, Mary. Quick. Let's get the others.'

So the brother and sister hurried back to the schoolhouse as fast as they could.

Despite the wailing of Jenny's pipes, Robbie Mcleod wasn't even properly awake when Jimmy and Mary Watson confronted him.

'Someone up there,' gasped Mary. 'On the crags.'

'Looks like men,' wheezed Jimmy. 'Two of them.'

'Whut? Whut?' cried Robbie. 'Tell me slowly. My head's in a dither at the minute.'

'Two people, up on the crags,' said Jimmy as slowly as he could. 'I think it's rescuers. It doesn't look like any of the parents.'

Robbie went to the boys' toilets and sloshed some water on his face before going to fetch Morag. He knew Alistair would want to be in on it too, but he was at the farm, and there just wasn't time to go and fetch him. Within a few minutes, a whole gang of children set out for the back of the glen. They pulled two sledges behind them and carried ropes taken from Heather Brown's general stores.

Once again, it was hard going, but they were determined to reach the two people. They didn't know whether they were alive or dead, but since there was always a chance they still breathed the children knew that the rescue had to take place immediately. Time was vitally important. The sooner the children could get the victims of the winter mountains into warm beds, the more chance they would have of surviving.

'If they're dead,' said Robbie in a voice that only wavered for a moment, 'we'll bury them under the snow. They'll stay gude and stiff until the thaw at least. But I hope they're not,' he added quickly.

'They might well be,' said Morag, battling beside him.

'Well, I just hope they're not,' said Robbie, 'for the sake of the wee 'uns. It's no nice to have dead bodies. It sort of – well, it clutters things up a bit.'

The ridge proved to be extremely difficult to ascend, as everyone guessed it would be. Jimmy Watson, Robbie Mcleod and Morag Knowehead formed a kind of chain, to help each other up the steep icy walls of the mountain. Several times they spoke about going back: many times they paused for breath and rest. However, they did struggle on, valiantly, until it became certain that they would reach the crag where the adults were lying.

When they reached the two bodies the children found they were men. The men were still alive, though not conscious. They felt extremely cold. The children heaved each man on to a sledge and tied him on with rope. Then they lowered the sledges, some holding on the back ropes and some pulling on the front ropes, down the mountain slope.

It took practically all day to get the men back to a dwelling. There the men were put in a double bed together in the minister's house, The Manse, which was the closest building to the back of the village. A fire was lit in their room and some hot soup was made. Morag set up teams of kids to watch over the two invalids. It was she who insisted that the men be forced to drink the hot soup, though the pair of them barely knew what was happening to them.

When all was quiet and the men were resting, she spoke to Robbie.

'Who do you think they are, Robbie? Do you think they came to rescue us?'

Robbie shook his head. 'Naw, why should they? No one kens the adults are gone. In any case, you wouldn't get anyone starting out to cross the Twa Bens in the raggedy clothes they're wearin' — not someone who kens what they're doing. These two have hardly got anythin' on, and just ordinary shoes, not climbing boots or anythin'. These two are just lost, so they are.'

'They could have been hunters,' said Morag.

Robbie frowned. 'Why d'you say that?'

'Because I found these in their pockets,' and she held out her hand. In it were two identical large clasp knives. Robbie took one and opened it. The blade was very sharp and about ten centimetres long. It certainly looked like a hunter's, or a fisherman's knife. He snapped it shut.

'They're not dressed like hunters,' said Robbie. 'Hunters are no so daft as to go out dressed like that, either. And where are the guns?'

'Maybe they dropped them somewhere, or threw them away when they got into trouble on the mountain. A gun's heavy, Robbie, and they wouldn't want to drag it around with them once they knew they were in trouble.'

Robbie nodded. 'That's true. Anyway, we'll ask them when they get a bit better. They'll soon tell us who they are.'

So the two sick men were spoonfed for the next two days, with children coming and going, the interest in their patients high. Morag was on duty, watching over the two souls, when the first of them came round. She had been busy poking the fire and came up to the bedside to see that one of the men had his eyes open.

They were both tall, thin men, but it was the pale one, with the black-rimmed, hollow eyes, that stared back at her. His close-cropped grizzled hair was unevenly cut, as if someone had chopped it off with a blunt knife. There were tufts of grey hair sprouting from his earholes and nose. His teeth were like pegs, stained brown, and two lower incisors were missing. A gnarled, raw hand came out from beneath the covers to scratch the coarse cracked skin just below his nose.

He began making a sucking sound with his teeth, as if they were painful and this somehow soothed them.

For a long time the dark, dead eyes bore into Morag's own, giving no hint of what kind of a man lay behind them, and a shiver of fear trickled through her.

Then he spoke.

'Where am I?' he croaked in a funny accent. 'What's all this, then? Who are you?'

'English, are you?' said Morag.

The man tried to go up on his elbows, but was obviously weak, and fell back down again.

He stared at the ceiling for a while, then spoke again in a quiet voice.

'Yeah, I'm English. Where are we?'

'You're in The Manse,' said Morag, tucking in the sheets in a busy and nurse-like manner.

'The Manse?'

'The minister's house, in Canlish Glen,' said Morag, thinking that perhaps the man wasn't a Christian, and might not know what a manse was.

'Canlish Glen,' repeated the man. 'It don't mean nothin' to me. I just remember being cold. Bloody cold. Where's McFee?'

'If you mean your friend, he's there beside you,' answered Morag.

'What? Are we in bed together?' He strained to look. 'How's that?'

'We found you on the mountainside,' said Morag. 'You're in there together for warmth. You nearly died. I think you'll be all right now, but you mustn't get up too soon.'

The man tried again to raise himself on to his elbows and this time he succeeded. He looked around the room staring at the dark strong furniture and seemed to notice the framed religious tract on the far wall. He looked down beside him at the threadbare rug on the wooden floorboards. Then he stared at Morag, who became uncomfortable under his gaze and went to poke the fire again, causing it to blaze. Finally he looked at the big round alarm clock on the table beside the bed.

'Minister's house, eh?' said the man. 'You're just a brat, though. You should be in bed at this time of night. Where's your old man? Where's your mum?'

'There are no adults here,' said Morag. 'Only children. The adults went away for the winter.'

'What, and left you kids to look after yourselves?'

'Aye and a good job we're making of it,' said Morag stoutly.

'Disgustin',' said the man. 'They ought to be horsewhipped.' He looked at the worn clothes piled neatly on one of the chairs and a strange expression crossed his face.

'Gimme that coat,' he said, harshly. 'Quick.'

There was a note of panic in his voice.

Morag handed him the coat to which he was pointing.

The man delved into the inside pocket and his hand came out with a soft leather pouch. When he opened it up, Morag could see bits of jewellery and shiny stones. The children had already seen the bundle, but had put it back where they found it. It was no concern of theirs what was in an adult's pocket. The man checked the contents of the pouch and then looked up at Morag again.

'Still here,' he grunted.

Morag bristled. 'Of course it's still there. What do you take us for, thieves?'

'You never know,' he said, taking out a silver coin. 'Here, this is for lookin' after us. Buy yourself somethin'.'

Morag made no move to touch the money.

'I don't want it,' she said. 'My father wouldn't like me to take money – or anything – from strangers. Not for helping people as we should do.'

The man shrugged. 'Suit yourself,' he said.

Then he stared again at the pile of clothes. 'What happened to our pistols?'

'Pistols?'

'Our guns?'

'Oh, you probably lost them on the mountain. I found these in your pocket, though,' and she held out the two knives.

'Give 'em to me,' he told her, holding out his hand.

She did so, but before she stepped back again, he grabbed her wrist in a strong tight grip. With his other hand he flicked open one of the clasp knives. His wizened, unshaven face came close to hers and Morag was overpowered by the smell of stale breath coming from his mouth. It made her feel ill. He brought the knife up, so that the light from the window caught the honed edge, which flashed silver.

'French-made, in Marseilles, of good steel. Nice piece of work, ain't it. Listen, pretty face, you better not be messin' me around,' he hissed into her face. 'If me pistol's here, you'd better tell me.'

He seemed very strong, despite the fact that he was ill, and his fingers dug into her arm like talons.

'I don't know what you're talking about,' cried Morag, frightened by his eyes. 'I don't know about any guns.'

'You better not,' murmured the man, dropping back on to the pillow.

Morag wrenched her arm away from him and backed towards the door, but before she had even reached it the man was asleep again, still clutching the open clasp-knife.

Morag went straight over to the schoolhouse and woke Robbie, to tell him what had occurred.

'I don't like that man,' said Morag. 'He was nasty to me. I didn't like his eyes. They were horrid. I don't want to look after those men any more.' Close to hysteria, she told Robbie what had happened.

Robbie tried to calm her down.

'Maybe it was because he thought you stole his gun? You know, people get a bit funny if they've been ill, don't they? They get sort of feverish and start ranting and raving. I'll go and watch them for a while.'

Robbie went over to The Manse and took up the vigil, but he was feeling by no means secure. The tale Morag had told him was worrying. Who were the two men, if they weren't lost hunters? He stared at the one with the knife, lying back with his mouth open and snoring. Then at the other one, whose longish, lank, black hair was dirtying the pillow with its grease. This one had a huge curved nose with a deep, terrible scar across the bridge, as if he'd been struck by an axe or something. They were both so angular and gaunt it seemed to Robbie they hadn't had a decent meal for a hundred years.

No, they don't look like hunters to me, he thought.

Chapter Six

TRUE COLOURS ARE REVEALED

They were all gathered in the school, a few days after the first man had opened his eyes. Only Elsbeth and Hamish Cairns were missing. They had remained at the farmhouse, having too many chores to do. The men had requested the assembly, wanting to meet everyone in the village, 'to thank them'. Since many of the children had not seen the men they were curious.

Both the men were now on their feet, their energy restored. They told the children their names were Tyler and McFee, and that they had been 'on the hills training with the army' when they were caught in a snowstorm. They became lost on the mountains, they said, and decided to head for the nearest village. They announced that the children had saved their lives and that they would be 'making a donation to the poor box', though they didn't say how much.

'We're not rich men, you understand,' said the one called Tyler, staring at them with his dark, hollow eyes, 'but we've got a tidy bit of boodle in our pockets . . .'

When they had stopped bragging, Morag asked simply, 'Which village were you heading for?'

The man called Tyler scratched his gaunt face, as if biding for time, and faltered, 'This one of course – er . . .'

'Canlish Glen,' Jimmy Watson prompted Tyler, thus earning for himself a glare from Morag. She had wanted to see if Tyler could remember it for himself.

'Er, yeah – Canlish Glen.'

Alistair said, 'If you're in the army, why are you wearing those clothes?'

'See, we dinna wear uniform a' the time,' the man called McFee replied in a strong West Lowlands accent. 'Not when we're in training, so tae speak.'

His strange, narrow head nodded as he spoke, the black hair flicking his stringy neck with its flails. His ears stuck out like sails on the side of his head. His huge, cleft nose added to the intensity to his eyes. His head gave the impression that it was fashioned of odd leftover features, hastily put together by a short-sighted creator.

'But,' insisted Alistair, 'you should surely wear clothing more suited to climbing mountains in the winter. You look like tramps out for a stroll in the park.'

Several children laughed at this and McFee gave Alistair a cold stare.

'We're practisin' being spies,' said McFee, eventually. 'You see, we have to pretend we've been sent into enemy territory, like in war, eh? So we wear these old clothes an' what-have-you, in case we get picked up by the enemy. No the *real* enemy, of course, just some other regiment boys, dressed up like, in uniforms. It's like the real thing, see? It's to train us as spies, for when we get sent behind the lines, eh?'

'Speakin' of which,' Tyler interrupted, 'where can we do some shoppin'? I dunno about you, McFee, but I need some warmer clothes. I'm damn well freezing.'

Jimmy Watson said, 'There's Mr Brown's store. You can buy some clothes there.'

'But no Mr Brown to pay, eh?' said McFee, smiling.

'You can pay me,' said Heather Brown. 'I'm managing the store until my parents come back again.'

Tyler laughed. 'Well, there's a thing, ain't it? No grown-ups anywhere in the village. Where'd you say they got to?'

'They all went away one night,' Jimmy told them, apparently happy to supply information to the two men, 'and we're stuck here on our own until the snow thaws.'

'Well, there's a thing,' Tyler repeated, and laughed again, casting a significant look at McFee. McFee didn't smile much. He nodded slowly, his face quite serious.

It was getting near evening. Alistair and Angel got up and walked towards the doorway.

Tyler shouted suddenly in a harder voice than he had been using until now, 'Where d'you think you're going, eh? Who said you could go anywhere?'

Alistair turned, alarmed by the tone the man was using.

'Back to the farm. The animals have to be fed. Elsbeth and Hamish can't do everything. I didn't know we had to ask permission . . .'

'Elsbeth and Hamish?' interrupted McFee. 'Ah thought ah told everyone to be here.'

'They can't leave the livestock,' said Angel, sharply. 'Don't you understand that?'

Tyler hunched in a threatening manner and gave Angel a dangerous look. The man suddenly reminded Alistair of a bird-eating spider he had once seen in a film, about to leap on a victim. Instinctively Alistair stepped back, away from Angel, then felt ashamed of himself for leaving her standing alone.

Tyler pointed a crooked finger and murmured in a low ugly tone. 'You watch your manners when you're talking to adults, madam. Now, this Elsbeth and Hamish – are they children?'

Alistair sighed. 'We told you, they're *all* children in the village at the moment. There isn't any grown-up around.'

'Just in case,' said Tyler, 'I think I'll go with you to this farm.'

'Just in case what, hen?' piped Robbie Mcleod, in a mocking tone.

'You shut yer mouth,' said McFee, pointing at Robbie. 'Ah don't want any insolence from any of you, understand me? Ah'll cut your heads off, so ah will.'

The whole mood of the meeting had suddenly changed. No longer were the men trying to smarm their way into the children's good books. There was an ugly atmosphere now. Alistair could see something in McFee's manner which frightened him very much. The man had a certain menace about him that would have scared an adult, let alone a young boy. It did not take much imagination to see that McFee could be a very dangerous individual if crossed by anyone. Certainly Robbie clamped up straight away and looked at his feet. Alistair didn't blame Robbie Mcleod for that, or think him a coward. He would have done the same.

'And another thing,' said Tyler, 'who's been makin' all that blasted noise with the bagpipes?'

Jenny, sitting cross-legged on the floor, stood up and raised her hand.

'You? Well, you can just stop, all right? It's enough to turn a man barmy.'

McFee stared at Tyler and said, 'There's nothin' wrong with the pipes.'

'There is with them pipes – they sound like a weasel bein' strangled.'

'Ah like the sound of the pipes,' said McFee in a dangerous voice. 'Ah like music.'

Tyler sniggered, 'Yeah, but this ain't *real* music you play on the piano, McFee. *I* like that too. This is just a bleedin' row. It's so damned *miserable*.'

'You, lassie,' said McFee to Jenny, 'when you play the pipes, play somethin' bright and breezy. None of that dreary stuff you've been playing. Ah dinna want to hear laments, y'ken? Somethin' a bit cheery, eh?'

Tyler stared at his partner for a moment, then nodded and laughed.

'All right, if that's the way McFee wants it – but I'm goin' to stuff wax in me ears. I'll have a look at the farm, McFee, while you listen to the pipes. I'll call in this shop on the way and get some decent clothes – a good pair of boots and a few thick shirts and things.'

Alistair, Morag and Robbie exchanged fearful glances. They had all wanted adults in the village, had wished for them desperately, and now there were adults here. But these were two adults the like of which the children had not seen before and they were quickly coming to the conclusion that it was better to have no adults than these two creatures. Tyler and McFee were like two wild beasts, let loose in a school playground.

There was another problem. If Jenny couldn't practise laments, she wouldn't be able to play a martial pibroch. This was a bad setback for the children. It was also evident that they had to be careful not to attract attention while searching for music. If Tyler and McFee became suspicious, they might put a stop to the quest for the pibroch altogether.

Robbie whispered to Jimmy, 'If you so much as say a word about the legend to these two, I'll *kill* you, Jimmy Watson, so I will.'

Jimmy nodded, slowly, without looking at Robbie. He whispered back, 'I'm not daft. I want them home too, but until then I'm going to be boss, Robbie Mcleod . . .'

'Stop talking there,' said McFee. 'Right, we'll

have supper ready, when you get back, Tyler, won't we, kids?'

No one answered him.

Tyler turned to Heather Brown.

'The keys, sweetie. Gimme the keys to the shop.'

Heather went red and clutched her pocket.

'GIMME THE DAMN KEYS!' yelled Tyler, his hand flashing forward and grabbing her by the throat.

Heather's hand came out of her pocket slowly and handed him the keys to the store. She began to cry. Mary Watson put an arm around her shoulders.

'Now listen, and listen good,' said Tyler, staring without compassion at Heather Brown. 'I'm tellin' you this for your own good, see. If me or McFee gives you an order, you do it, and quick, or there'll be trouble. We don't want to have to shout at you all the time – it makes me throat sore. And I don't want to hurt you – much – but McFee's got a shorter temper than me and he likes hitting things. Just do as you're told and we'll get along nicely. If you give us any trouble, you'll regret it, because we ain't bleedin' little drummer boys. I'll kick your backsides from here to the North Pole, you understand me?'

No one replied.

'He said,' McFee growled in a quiet tone, 'do you no understand him?'

There were murmurs of 'aye' and 'yes' from various children in the room.

'Gude,' said McFee. 'Now we've got that straight, how about getting some food on the go?

70

Who was the leader here, afore we came?'

'I was,' said Robbie. 'Me and Morag.'

McFee gave Robbie a hard look. 'Well, you're no leader now, get it? You're the one who's full o' blasted mouth. Where's that other kid . . .' McFee looked around the room, his eyes finally resting on Jimmy Watson. 'See you,' continued McFee, 'you're the leader now, right?'

Jimmy smiled, looking around the room at the faces of the other children. Robbie was glaring at him, but Robbie didn't matter any longer. Now the adults were here, Robbie couldn't touch him without reprisal.

McFee said to Jimmy, 'Get them started.'

'All right,' said Jimmy, 'Robbie, you set to and peel the potatoes . . .'

'In a pig's eye . . .' Robbie began, but when he caught McFee's stare, he stopped and scowled, then made his way towards the sack of potatoes in the corner of the room.

Alistair and Angel left with Tyler.

The first thing Tyler did was visit the general store, where he helped himself to some proper winter clothes and boots. He then looked around him, at the Aladdin's cave of general goods. Next he inexplicably filled his pockets with shiny nails, screws and boot studs; gathered all the packets of tobacco and a few briar pipes; found a sheath knife and stuck it in his belt; grabbed handfuls of trinkets; took a wicker basket and filled it with soap, bottles of cheap perfume and flimsy women's headscarves. He obviously thought at one time about taking an axe, but put it down when it appeared to be too heavy.

The man's demeanour worried Alistair. Now that they were in Mr Brown's store Tyler's normally empty eyes became feverish. His hands became twitchy. Ignoring the two children he kept glancing around him greedily. Alistair guessed what Tyler was thinking: everything in the store was there for the taking. Alistair could see the man gauging what was small and valuable, so that he could transfer it to his greatcoat pockets.

Tyler went from shelf to shelf, assessing and sometimes taking items, until he was so loaded down he could hardly squeeze behind the counter.

Finally he turned to Alistair and said, 'Where's the grog, young 'un?'

'Grog?'

'The whisky. Where is it? You're not telling me there's no whisky in a Scotch village?'

Alistair wanted to scream at this Sassenach, '*Scottish* village, not *Scotch*', but instead he feigned ignorance.

'I dinna ken,' he said.

Tyler lowered his head and his eyes narrowed.

'If I find you're lyin' to me, you little Jock, I'll break your neck, you understand me?'

'I dinna ken where any whisky is.'

Angel shook her head too.

Both children knew that all the liquor was kept in the cellar of the store, under a trapdoor behind the counter. Mr Brown kept a mat over the trapdoor, to stop flour and other finely ground goods from falling through the cracks. Neither Alistair nor Angel was going to tell Tyler anything.

Tyler began turning over boxes and looking under barrels. He found nothing and began to get angry.

'There'll be whisky in the houses, right? I'll go look for it later. Let's get to this farm of yours.'

Tyler carefully locked up the store after he left and put the key in his pocket.

'Can't have you lot thievin' from the place, can we?' he said jocularly.

They made their way through the snow, with Tyler staggering under the load he was carrying. Finally the thief stopped and said, 'I can't carry all this junk on my own. You two will have to help me. Here, take some.'

Alistair and Angel were given the basket full of stolen items to carry.

When they arrived at the farm, Tyler took them all back again.

Hamish came out to meet them.

'You're late,' he said. 'We've got to muck out the cowshed, Alistair.'

'I know, I'm sorry,' Alistair replied, 'but we couldn't get away.'

Tyler said to Hamish, 'You're a cocky little swine, aren't you? Who are you ordering around, eh?'

Hamish blinked and stared at the man whose pockets were bulging and whose face was red with the exertion of walking.

'Ah'm just saying to Alistair here, that we've got to get the cowshed mucked out.'

'I *heard* what you said, sailor,' smirked Tyler, 'I was just remarkin' on the *way* you said it. Go on then, go and muck out the shed. I'll have a good look round while you're doing that. Has your dad got any whisky?'

Hamish shook his head quickly.

'My father doesn't drink. The minister doesn't like drinking in the village.'

'Oh, doesn't he?' cried Tyler. 'Well, the minister's going to get a shock when he comes back, ain't he? Which brings to mind somethin' else. We ain't really established where the grown-ups have gone to, have we?'

'We don't know for sure. We just woke up one morning and they were gone.'

'Sounds like a fairy story to me,' said Tyler.

'Well, it's the truth. They went off into the mountains, between the Twa Bens.'

Tyler stared at the surrounding peaks, wearing their formidable white-pointed caps like an uneven row of château towers. He noted their sheer icy slopes, their snowy chasms, their snowbound passes. If the adults of the village had gone up into those mountains, and hadn't returned in a day, then they were never coming down.

'Why did they go up?' Tyler asked. 'Someone lost up there? Some sort of search goin' on?'

'Something like that,' replied Hamish, weary of talking with this brutal stranger.

'Maybe some travellers got lost,' muttered Tyler.

It struck Tyler that mountains must be a source of boodle. Travellers carried valuables with them. It must be like an elephant's graveyard up there. There would be undiscovered corpses stuck in crevices, down potholes, in caves, and over cliffs. If you had knowledge of the mountains, you could find and strip the bodies.

And if *he* thought that way, why not a few shabby villagers thinking the same. Yes, that must have been it. Someone, or a group of people, lost in the mountains, and the whole village turned out to reap the prizes. All except the children of a certain age, who would have been left asleep in bed.

As Tyler followed Angel into the house, Hamish yelled something in Gaelic.

Tyler came out again straight away. 'What was that?'

He bent down over Hamish like a grizzled predatory bird, as if ready to peck into his head.

'What was what?' asked Hamish.

'What you said. What kind of language is that? Double Dutch?'

'Naw, it's Gaelic. I was just telling my sister that a stranger was entering the house. It's the custom.'

Tyler sniffed hard, the shaggy nostril hairs disappearing for a moment. He made a clucking sound with his tongue as he continued to stare at Hamish's head. Finally, he spoke again, in a low dangerous voice.

'You can keep that kind of language to yourself, sailor, because I don't like to hear it.'

With that, the man sucked in his already hollow cheeks, then straightened up again. He turned and went indoors, the crack of his boot soles resounding on the stone floor of the kitchen.

Hamish said to Alistair as they made their way to the cowshed, 'What's happened?'

'I think we've got stuck with a couple o' bad

'uns,' said Alistair quietly, as if he were afraid that Tyler might be listening. 'That one's just robbed Mr Brown's store. What was it you shouted to Elsbeth?'

Hamish's peaky little face looked up into Alistair's and the farmer's son tapped his temple.

'I told her to hide the shotgun in her bed. Ah'm no daft, am I, Alistair Burns?'

Alistair smiled. 'You're no daft, Hamish Cairns.'

The pair of them cleaned out the shed and stables. They collected all the eggs they could find in the barn and put the chickens and ducks away for the night. Finally they fed the pigs. Myrtle went for Alistair again and he had to keep jumping up on the sty wall to escape her. It almost became a game, except that Alistair knew if the old sow got his ankle, he would regret playing with her.

With the darkness around them and their hurricane lamps burning, the two boys completed their tasks, then went back to the kitchen. They were happy to see that Tyler had gone. Elsbeth was upset because Tyler had been through all the drawers and cupboards in the house and had taken a gold wedding ring bequeathed to her mother by her grandmother.

There was not a great deal of value in the farmhouse, because most of the wealth was in the livestock. They had no silver teasets, nor hoards of cash. They were hard-working farmers, with very little to fall back on. Which was why it was so important that Hamish and Elsbeth kept the farm ticking over, until their parents returned.

Later that night, as they lay in their beds, they heard the sound of music.

'What's that?' called Hamish from his room.

Alistair remembered what Tyler had said about McFee playing the piano.

'I think it's one of the men,' he called back. 'Playing the minister's piano.'

The music was jaunty, belying the personality of the man whose gnarly fingers produced it. Alistair lay and listened, unable to do anything else. Instead of cheering him up, the merry sounds created a feeling of dread in Alistair.

Alistair searched his mind for a word to describe it – a word which the minster sometimes used – aye, that was it – such jovial music coming from one such as McFee was like the Devil's laughter – profane.

Chapter Seven

McFEE AND THE SHOTGUN

When Tyler and McFee had satisfied themselves that there were no adults in the village, and that the children had no way of escaping and raising the alarm, the two thieves settled into a nice comfortable life. They slept in separate rooms at The Manse and expected to be waited on hand and foot.

On a typical day the men would rise at noon, after being brought a mug of tea in bed. Sometimes Tyler was up earlier, but never before ten o'clock. This at least gave the children some respite from his bullying and time to search for the music of the Phantom Piper's pibroch.

McFee and Tyler made it plain that they thought it quaint that the children should be trying to run the village just as if they were adults.

One Sunday, when the children were gathered in the kirk and going through their very shortened version of the service, the men came and stood at the back. They joined in lustily with the hymns but the children knew they were being mocked. During the prayers, the men just talked to each other in normal voices, making it difficult for the children to concentrate. Besides, the kids had one very important prayer, for the return of the adults, which they did not like to say in front of the men.

After the fifteen-minute service, the men made plain their contempt for the worship.

'Bakin' the bread's fine,' laughed Tyler, 'we got to eat – but takin' a church service? I mean . . . it's blooming sacrilege, ain't it? Kids doing that stuff? You don't even know the right words to use. I should stick to shopkeepin' and baking bread if I was you lot.'

'What's the good of school? How can you learn,' said McFee, 'when ye dinna ken your face fra the back o' yer head?'

'We're making sure we don't grow up as ignorant as you two,' Morag retorted.

McFee stepped forward quickly and slapped her face.

'Talk to *me* like that, missy, and you'll feel the flat o' mah hand more than once.'

Morag stared back, red-faced but defiant, and refused to burst into tears. The marks of McFee's fingers appeared on her cheek. Robbie Mcleod made a little sound and bunched his fists, but McFee just smiled at him.

'Aye, boy?' he sneered.

'You wait until my father comes back,' Morag said. 'He'll make you pay for that.'

McFee laughed at this and then, seeing the organ, sat down at it.

'Awa' and pump the bellows, lassie,' he ordered.

Morag did as she was told: defying McFee once in a day was trouble enough.

When there was sufficient air, McFee began to play a fugue and Morag was astonished at the way his wiry fingers moved over the keys. His touch was delicate and sure, and he played with supreme confidence. The kirk was filled with the rousing sound of the music. When he had finished playing, he smirked, and sauntered out of the kirk as if he had just performed a miracle for the children.

'Nae more services,' he called back. 'There'll be workin' on the sabbath tae . . .'

The work of which the men approved was closely related to their stomachs. The baking of the bread was considered by them to be essential. Their interest in the farm was mostly in chickens, eggs, milk and cheese. They marched into the store and the sweetshop and took what they wanted, when they wanted it, so saw no reason for Heather Brown or Morag Knowehead to be behind the counters.

If the children were not doing something useful, like providing fresh food, then they should fetch and carry for them.

Not only did the two men make the children serve their every need, they expected to be entertained also. They would play most games, from draughts to snakes and ladders, but the one game they loved to play the most was cards. They played each other of course, but to make the game more interesting they also taught one or two of the children how to gamble.

The money they played with came from the

houses in the village. Tyler and McFee had systematically robbed every house, going through drawers, cupboards, sideboards and even looking under mattresses. They took every coin they could find, even old Jock Walker's nest egg of golden guineas, passed on to him by his grandfather. He had kept them in a flour sack in his cellar because he didn't trust banks.

Tyler and McFee ignored any paper money. Jewellery was their favourite loot. They took every necklace, bracelet and set of earrings they could find, whether they were actually worth anything or not. Sometimes they dished coin money out to Robbie, Alistair and Jimmy, so that the older boys could play cards with them.

However, the longer Robbie and Alistair played, the better they became, until finally they were winning almost every game. The men then simply began cheating after a while and won all their losses back that way.

Jimmy did not try to win. He was happy to let the two men have their own way so long as he remained their favourite amongst the children. Jimmy liked being the leader, telling people what to do, and using the threat of Tyler or McFee if someone disobeyed him. The men in their turn saw it was useful to have one of the children as their puppet despot.

Mary still passed on all the gossip to Jimmy, for he was still her brother and she loved him as such, and Jimmy in turn told Tyler and McFee what was passing between the children. Any plots they hatched against the men, were soon discovered by Jimmy and passed on to either Tyler or McFee.

Robbie was always fuming under his breath at Jimmy.

'You wait, Watson,' he breathed. 'I'll sort you out soon enough when the time comes.'

But until that time Jimmy was the king of the heap. He was the puppet ruler of Canlish Glen. What he said was law, backed up by the strength and might of Tyler and McFee, and anyone who disagreed with him was quickly taken to task by one or both of the men. Jimmy was now able to control Robbie for the first time in his life and it felt good to him. Robbie had been the master, now it was Jimmy's turn.

In fact, Robbie had been no fairer, except that he had not been backed up by adults. One or two of the kids even preferred Jimmy, because he was more intelligent. Robbie tended to let fly with his fist, impulsively, while at least Jimmy reasoned with those who disobeyed, before finally going to the thieves and getting their support. His arrogance, however, was more openly on display than Robbie's had ever been, and the children above all hated the way he was lording it over them and gloating at the same time.

One day Jimmy, Robbie, Alistair and Tyler were playing cards at The Manse. McFee was sleeping upstairs. Jimmy turned to Tyler and said, 'Where do you come from? How did you get on the side of the mountain?'

Both Robbie and Alistair looked up and stared at Tyler, waiting for his answer.

Tyler raised his eyes from his cards and stared at Jimmy.

'Come from?' he repeated.

'Yes,' said Jimmy. 'I mean, I know you're English, and McFee is a Scot, but whereabouts are you from? How did you get to know McFee?'

'Damn silly question,' muttered Tyler, his eyes taking on a faraway look. 'Come from? Why, we came . . .' His brow furrowed as if he were concentrating, trying to recall something. 'Why, we was on – yes, we was on a north road – at least, *I* was. Then I met McFee. We did some thievin' one night. That was some time ago . . .' He seemed to drift off into a reverie. 'Yeah, that's it, on a road north, I think.'

Jimmy was not prepared to let it rest at that.

'North to where? Where were you going?'

'To fight,' said Tyler. 'Why else?' He riffled through his cards. 'Yeah, to damn well *fight*.'

Jimmy said excitedly, 'Who – to fight who?'

Tyler looked up and smiled now, a strange kind of smile, as if there were some secret behind it all. 'Why, each other, of course.' He let out a raucous laugh and slapped his thigh. 'Yes, that was it – we were going to fight each other.'

'Yes, but weren't you in the army together?'

A distant light suddenly came into Tyler's eyes.

'The army, but not together – yeah – why, I remember! We robbed some corpses on a battlefield. McFee likes to conveniently forget that, don't he? I can't remember exactly where it was. Anyway, we got a bit of boodle. Just went round pickin' the bodies, before the crows got to 'em. Dead horses there too – all bloated with the heat. Some of 'em had saddlebags with stuff worth

83

having. We made a good bit . . .'

He seemed to drift away somewhere, on a sea of thoughts.

'But how did you get here?' insisted Jimmy.

Tyler's eyes came into focus. He blew down his nostrils furiously. He scratched his grey tufted hair and glared at Jimmy. 'What? How the hell do I know.' he snapped. 'You ask too many questions. It's not good for you.'

Jimmy let the subject drop, but Alistair and Robbie continued to stare at Tyler, until he told them to 'look at somethin' else'.

After the game was over and they were walking away from The Manse – Jimmy had stayed with Tyler – Robbie said to Alistair, 'What did you make of that? When Jimmy asked him those questions.'

Alistair said, 'He doesna seem to ken where he comes from, does he?'

'Who?'

'Tyler – he doesn't seem to know where his home is or how he got on to the side of the mountain. He seems all mixed up.'

'Maybe he's got a bad memory?' suggested Robbie.

'Aye,' replied Alistair, 'that – or he really *doesn't* know the answer.'

Robbie said what was actually in Alistair's mind.

'Maybe they came out of nowhere – like our parents went into nowhere?'

'That's what I think,' said Alistair, nodding seriously. 'Have you noticed how sometimes they seem old-fashioned and other times they seem, well, up to date? Look at the way they treat paper money. They don't take any interest in it at *all*. What I mean to say is, they don't put any value on it, but they don't say, 'Look at these funny five-pound notes,' either. It's as if . . .' Alistair searched for the right words. 'It's as if they didn't belong *anywhere*, if you know what I mean. They're sort of just bad men from any time or place . . .'

Robbie's brow furrowed. 'That's a bit deep for me, Alistair Burns, but I think I ken what you're saying. In which case we've got to watch them closely. If they came from nowhere, then they know how to get back there. They must hold the key to the gates of nowhere. Y'ken?'

'Aye,' Alistair replied. 'But we'll keep this a secret between you an' me, eh? It'll only worry the bairns.'

'Agreed,' replied Robbie. 'Except Morag – we've got to tell Morag.'

'Aye, of course. One thing's sure though, wherever they came from, they're bad from head to foot. D'you think they would kill one of us, Robbie?'

'I'm certain sure they would,' said Robbie, grimly, unable to suppress a shudder. 'Have you seen their eyes?'

Alistair recalled the dark-ringed hollow eyes of Tyler and the cadaverous eyes of McFee, and he too shivered.

'I don't think it would bother them one bit,' he agreed.

They went to look for Morag and tell her what they had talked over.

At the farm, things went on as usual. Although

the men required Alistair's presence for cards every so often, he still worked with Hamish at keeping the farm going. One day McFee turned up unexpectedly on the doorstep. The two boys were out exercising the cart-horse in a nearby field. Elsbeth and Angel were busy around the chickens and ducks.

'Ah've just thought to mahsel',' said McFee to the girls, 'that ah wouldna mind a gude bit of rabbit stew for ma supper. Your old man must have some snares about the house, eh? What farmer doesn't have a few traps. Now don't you bother, ah'll find them mahsel'.'

He did not find any snares, but he did find the shotgun where Hamish had hidden it. He also found a box of cartridges. McFee was delighted with himself. 'A gun,' he said in a satisfied tone.

He played with the shotgun, ascertaining how to break it open. He stared down the silver double barrels, then he snapped it shut again. Cocking the weapon, he pulled the triggers, smiling at the girls when the hammers clacked against the empty breech. Then he used his clasp knife to cut open and inspect one of the cartridges, noting the wadding, the pellets and the powder. It was as if he were on a voyage of discovery, but one which was faintly familiar to him, in the same way that a man who was used to firing a longbow might set out to understand the principles behind a crossbow.

He held up one of the cartridges. 'Is this it?' he asked, then managed to load the gun after one or two abortive tries.

'It's in gude condition,' he murmured.

'Of course it is,' said Elsbeth. 'It's my father's.'

McFee stared at her and said, 'Ay, well,' then aimed at her head along the blue-metal barrels, laughing when she winced and moved out of the way. He traced the centripetal designs around the hammers with his finger and admired the worn but polished wooden stock. Then he whipped it up to his shoulder once or twice and pretended to fire at a running hare through the window.

'Now ah can do a wee bit o' hunting, eh, girls? Blow a few rabbits in the air. Grab me a few grouse.'

He went off with the weapon, into the pine forest behind the farm, and later they heard one or two muffled reports.

Hamish was very upset when he came home to find the gun missing.

'It's my father's,' he kept saying. 'They'd better no damage my father's gun.'

But the children all knew that the real reason Hamish had wanted to keep the shotgun hidden was because the men would be twice as dangerous with it.

The following day, McFee was back again. All four children were at home. He marched into the farmhouse kitchen and demanded a cup of tea. Then he kicked the snow from his boots against the grate and sat down. He put the shotgun on the table.

Once the tea had been brought, McFee turned to Hamish and said, 'Get me a saw – for cutting steel.'

Instead of saying that there was no hacksaw at the farm, as he should have done, Hamish said, 'What for?'

'Don't ask me questions,' growled McFee. 'Just do as you're telt.'

The steam from the tea wafted up around his face, giving it a ghoulish appearance, like some gaunt ethereal creature staring out through the mists.

Hamish went off to look for the hacksaw, while Alistair, Elsbeth and Angel were left to entertain McFee. They had found the best way to deal with the thief was to ask him about the robberies he had done. McFee was not loath to talk about such things. It furnished him something for his ego to brag about. He loved to call himself 'a strong man' and kept describing the violence he had used on his victims, to extort their money from them, or simply to feed his own amusement.

'There's rich people enough in the world,' he kept saying. 'Ah'm just helpin' to spread the money a bit.'

Hamish returned with a hacksaw.

McFee stood up by the kitchen table and put the shotgun down with the barrels sticking over the edge.

'Hold the gun down,' he ordered Alistair, 'while ah do the cuttin'.'

'What are you doing?' cried Hamish, pushing at McFee. 'That's my father's gun.'

'See you, you little runt,' snapped McFee, grabbing Hamish by the collar and lifting him off the floor. 'If ah have any more trouble from you,

88

you'll be through that window.'

Elsbeth cried, 'Please put him down, McFee.'

McFee gave Hamish a teeth-rattling shake and then plonked him back on the kitchen floor again.

There were tears in Hamish's eyes, but they were tears of anger, not of fear. However, he wisely went out of the room, not wanting to see his father's expensive weapon wilfully damaged.

Alistair had to hold the gun still, while McFee sawed a length off the barrels.

The hacksaw made a screeching sound cutting through the tempered steel which put Alistair's teeth on edge. He had difficulty in holding the shotgun still and once or twice McFee spoke to him sharply. Finally the barrels parted in two and the loose metal tubes fell to the stone farmhouse floor, chinking as they struck and rolled, making Black Gip jump and move away from his place by the kitchen range.

Once the barrels were shortened McFee cut the end off the rosewood stock, so that it was about half the size.

'That's better,' said McFee, holding up the now stubby weapon. 'That'll fit inside mah coat now.'

Alistair said, 'But the pellets won't go as far now – you won't be able to hunt rabbits with it.'

McFee looked at him. 'Who said ah won't?'

'It's not a matter of who says,' replied Elsbeth. 'It's a matter of physics. Did you no go to school?'

'Fizzicks? Whut's Fizzicks got to do with it?' cried McFee. 'It's easier to carry round like this.'

Elsbeth answered patiently, 'You need the long length of the barrels to keep the pellets tightly bunched and to make them go a further distance. Now you've sawn off the barrels they'll go every which-way and drop to the ground. If you'd kept the barrels on, it would shoot about thirty metres, but you'll be lucky if you can get half that distance now.'

McFee's eyes narrowed.

He looked at the shotgun, then he stared back at Elsbeth.

'Ah don't believe you,' he said. 'You're lyin'.'

McFee himself would lie just to make a point, but Elsbeth was not given to telling untruths. She stared back at McFee, the gulf of understanding between them too huge for either of them to make the leap.

'Why would I want to lie?' she asked him. 'I've got no reason.'

'You just want to make me look stupid,' snarled McFee.

Alistair butted in again here. 'She's telling the truth,' he said. 'You ask Hamish.'

McFee shouted, 'Hamish! Come here!'

Hamish came into the room a few moments later looking sullen.

McFee said, 'Listen, brat, see whut ah've done to your precious father's gun. Your sister seems to think it's damaged.'

'It's useless now,' shouted Hamish. 'Can't you see that? You've destroyed the choke.'

'The choke?' McFee said, in a quieter voice now.

'Aye,' said Hamish, 'the way the gun narrows to the holes at the end of the barrels – so the shot stays in a tight bunch when it comes out.'

'It'll no shoot sae far?'

'Useless,' confirmed Hamish, 'unless you're standing right on top o' something.'

McFee left the farmhouse in a bad temper, stalking back through the deep snow towards the school.

'Well,' said Hamish, staring at the severed barrels and stock end disgustedly. 'That's my father's gun ruined all right. I'm supposed to look after things while he's gone. Now look what's happened.'

'It's no your fault,' said Angel. 'You're only a boy. You canna fight a man.'

Hamish was worried about his father's reaction. Mr Cairns was not the best of dads when it came to showing affection, and the only time Hamish received any praise was when he did a job precisely as his father would have done it. Farmer Cairns was an exacting man, who was fond of saying that he did not suffer fools gladly. An arrogant statement, especially coming from a man whose very blinkered views on what was right and wrong made him the worst kind of fool.

Mr Cairns made no allowance for his son's age, or his daughter's love of riding – a pastime he considered frivolous – and spent his time trying to make them into perfect replicas of himself and his wife.

The children's mother suffered under the same oppressive criticism. She was told how to cut vegetables, how to roast meat, how to sew clothes, how to practise economy, all by a man who had no skill in any of these things except perhaps the last. Farmer Cairns was good at economising, on things like toys and dresses and jam and sweets and holidays.

Dinsie had been given to Farmer Cairns in part-payment of a debt and he had taken the animal thinking that she would make a good trap pony. It had been his wife's idea to give the creature to Elsbeth and when he had been nagged enough by both females he finally agreed. It was an action he later told everyone he regretted.

Elsbeth knew what her brother was thinking. She put her arm around the ten-year-old farm boy's shoulders and gave him a hug. It was the only thing she could do which meant anything at all. Hamish nodded slowly, then went out to feed the pigs. Only Elsbeth knew that it was not the shotgun Hamish cared about, it was the violation of his father's property,

Elsbeth was also indignant about the whole business, but she was a little older than Hamish and a lot more mature. She guessed that anger had no more effect on people like McFee than did common sense. Men of McFee's and Tyler's stamp were unreachable and evil.

Later that day, Alistair went out for a walk amongst the pines, as he often did of an evening. Once he was amongst the silence of the trees, for the third time since the adults had disappeared, he thought he heard something, deep in the heart of the highlands.

Some people say that silence is the loudest noise of all, because everyone can hear it, but down below the hush were the now familiar faint sounds of gathering clans: the running feet, the jingle of weapons, the rallying cries of chieftains calling their warriors to arms. Nothing was clear – just a vagueness of sound amongst the hills and glens, which drifted over the silent landscape, through the gaps in the mountains.

Alistair listened hard, straining his ears, as he thought he heard the sound of a lonely piper. It wasn't Jenny. The notes were far too confident for her to be playing. Alistair tried desperately to hear a melody in the sound, a tune that he could whistle to Sadie, for he was sure that the pibroch for which they were searching was out there, in the highlands, rather than on some page of a music book. He felt sure it *was* the highlands, the spirit of the landscape, which was responsible for the music that had enticed his mother from her bed, and had the whole adult population of Canlish marching to its beat.

'Please . . .' he whispered to the trees.

But he couldn't hold the music in his head and once the piper had ceased playing, the tune was lost to him.

Chapter Eight

ROBBIE McLEOD RUNS FOR IT

Robbie Mcleod was missing.

It was Jimmy who raised the alarm at ten o'clock in the morning and informed Tyler that Robbie Mcleod was nowhere to be found. McFec was still fast asleep in the next room and his snores could be heard, coming through the thick walls of the manse.

'I woke up this morning,' said Jimmy, 'and Robbie was gone. I think he's run off!'

Tyler's foul temper, a natural consequence of being woken up, was not improved by the news. He climbed wearily out of a bed with blankets and no sheets, scowling when his feet touched the freezing cold lino. His eyes were sore and watery. His nose felt lumpy. He ran his hands over the stubble on his face, through his grizzled hair, and then stared at Jimmy.

'Whaddya mean, gone?'

In the distance Jenny was playing the bagpipes and the sound began to grate on Tyler's nerves.

'Gone where?' he said.

'Just gone. He must have run away in the night.'

Tyler let this sink in for a few moments. Where would he go to? He couldn't get out of the valley, could he? What if he did? What if by some miracle the brat managed to reach the outside. How long would it be before outsiders got to Canlish Glen?

'All right, Jimmy. Leave this to me.'

Jimmy nodded and went away, while Tyler got dressed. Tyler decided not to wake McFee, who would take ages to bring himself round. In any case, McFee might kill the boy in his temper, and that wouldn't help things at all. It was simply a matter of getting the brat to come back again.

Jimmy was still waiting outside the bedroom when Tyler emerged, his bleary eyes now a little clearer.

'Go and get me McFee's shotgun,' he said to the boy. 'I need it.'

Jimmy gulped. 'You're – you're no going to shoot Robbie Mcleod, are you?'

'Not so long as he does what I tell him,' replied Tyler, steely-eyed. Then he stared at Jimmy and said, 'Nah, just scare 'im a little. Go and get me McFee's gun, but don't wake him, mind. Just fetch it without disturbing him.'

Once the shotgun was in his possession, Tyler dressed as warmly as he could. Then he set out after the runaway Robbie, following the tracks from the school. Instead of heading north for the pass, Robbie's footprints led away from the village, to the south, behind the farm. In that direction Tyler could see a high steep ridge covered in pine trees. The face of the ridge was surely much too sheer to climb in winter, when the handholds would be iced over? There must be something about that ridge, thought Tyler, which the brat knows about.

Tyler could not understand why Robbie ever thought he stood even the remotest chance of escape that way. The closer the man came to the ridge, the more impossible it looked to climb. Apart from stunted firs growing from cracks in the rock which lay under the snow, there were no points which could be used to ascend the wall of ice and snow.

By the time Tyler actually reached the face, a snowstorm had begun rolling in. The wind was cutting round the crags so keenly that the flecks of snow it brought with it stung Tyler's cheeks. He was half-tempted to turn around and go back to the schoolhouse. Blizzards scared him. They seemed so mindlessly powerful. Tyler thought about the roaring fire in the schoolroom. He did not think himself unusual for wanting to be sitting in front of such a fire, instead of risking death by freezing.

The only thing that kept him there, searching, was the thought that Robbie might, by some miracle, get through to the outside world, the *real* world. Tyler wasn't absolutely sure what would happen to him and McFee if outsiders did get to know of what was going on in Canlish Glen, but he instinctively felt that it would not be to their advantage. He and McFee were part of some delicate unnatural bubble that could be burst by an intrusion from the world beyond the mountains. His cryptic feelings indicated that if they could remain isolated for long enough – enveloped by the ageless mountains – the situation would be permanent. It might remain so for ever.

Tyler entered a forest of pines that ran parallel to the ridge. It was darker and much gloomier inside. However, being one of the new silent forests of conifers which choke their undergrowth, there were no brambles or bushes to impede his progress. He moved in the eerie dimness on a soft carpet of pine needles, the canopy of evergreens above too dense even to allow snow through to the forest floor. Then he heard a noise. It came from a small glade below an overhang of the cliff: a clatter of loose stones. He stopped and listened. There was no doubt in his mind: someone was moving around in a gully at the base of the ridge.

Creeping forward, towards the greater light of the clearing, Tyler smiled grimly to himself. He would give the brat such a scare it would put him off running away ever again. It was tempting to fire the shotgun in the air – that would make the brat jump out of his skin – except that with the overhang the sound might cause an avalanche. He told himself he was not as stupid as some people believed. He knew how to think ahead. He knew how to survive in the wilds.

When he reached the edge of the clearing, Tyler listened again, and heard more sounds. It was too gloomy to see much, but there was a dark shape ahead. Tyler filled his lungs with breath, then went charging into the clearing, yelling like crazy and waving the shotgun in the air.

The next moment he saw a huge giant hurtling towards him, plunging through the lower branches of the trees, whipping some aside, snapping a few of them. The creature's head was down and a vast array of weapons pointed dangerously at Tyler's chest. The beast's coat was red, its eyes wide and full of fear, and clouds snorted from its nostrils as if forced through by a bellows. Its wild hooves thudded on the earth.

It was a great red stag, caught in a gully, and it intended to escape — over Tyler's dead body if necessary.

Tyler gave out a yell and threw himself sideways, dropping the shotgun. One of the points of the wide spread of antlers grazed his cheek in passing. He felt the hot breath of the stag on his face and smelled the thick coarse winter coat of the powerful beast. Then it thundered past him, into the trees, zig-zagging between the trunks until it was out of sight.

Tyler lay where he was in the snow for a few moments. His skin prickled with the shock of his narrow escape. There was sweat on his previously cold brow. Beneath his ribs his heart pounded swiftly. Having cornered and startled the stag, while it was up against the cliff face, Tyler had almost been impaled on the beast's antlers. If he had not thrown himself sideways in time, those enormous branches of horn would have smashed through his chest into his heart and lungs. He would have been left to bleed his life out on to the white snows of the forest.

Finally, he climbed unsteadily to his feet, his legs still shaking. He retrieved his gun from the snow. It took a lot of effort to walk on, but eventually he did so, still sticking to the base of the cliff where

Robbie's footprints had left a tell-tale trail. Tyler was now even more determined to get the boy. He had disturbed the monarch of the glen and nearly lost his life. There was something exhilarating in that fact.

Tyler had never seen an animal as big as that stag, not in the wild. It made him think about other creatures of the forest. He knew there were foxes and wildcats around, but what about wolves? A pack of wolves wouldn't run away. They would probably attack you and rip you apart.

Tyler shuddered at the thought.

He went on through the snow cautiously, staring around him every so often, making sure nothing was sneaking up on him. He rounded another spur and as he was creeping along the cliff bottom on the other side, something small struck him on the head. He thought at first that it might be bird lime and wiped his head quickly. Then he looked up.

There were no birds to be seen. What Tyler did see was Robbie Mcleod, halfway up the side of the cliff. Tyler recognised the vague dark shape through the swirling snowflakes. The boy was using a zigzag rock chimney – a lightning crack up the face of the cliff wide enough to crawl inside – to ascend.

Tyler stared at the boy for a moment and then shouted, 'Hey, brat, don't be daft – you'll kill yourself. There's a storm comin' up. You'll never make it – where'd'you think you're goin'? You'll fall and die, you stupid brat.'

Robbie stopped scrambling up the chimney, which looked like hard slow work, and stared down at Tyler. But the thirteen-year-old said nothing and after a while continued to climb. Tyler cursed him and shook his fist.

'If you don't come down here now, Robbie boy, I'll blow you off the cliff with this . . .'

Tyler now waved the gun in the air.

Robbie called back, 'You can't, you stupid Sassenach! McFee sawed the barrels off the gun. It'll no shoot more than a few metres at the most.'

Tyler stared at the stubby-looking gun in his hand. He was feeling annoyed now, as well as bitterly cold. The brat had to be brought down somehow.

Robbie was a liability.

Tyler sighed and lodged the shotgun in a crack between two rocks. Then he squeezed himself into the narrow rock chimney and began climbing up it after Robbie. Robbie, seeing him coming, started to move more quickly. It became a scrambling race between the man and the boy, with the very real danger of one of them falling out of the chimney and down the cliff.

The man, however, proved much the stronger climber. He was taller and could reach the handholds without straining. Tyler was also the more determined of the two. So he was the swifter.

After about ten minutes, Tyler was almost at the spot where Robbie was struggling to pull himself up a vertical part of the chimney. Given time Robbie could probably have made it, but there was no time: Tyler was right on his tail. Just as Robbie started to haul himself up the neck of the chimney, Tyler reached out and grabbed his ankle, holding him fast.

'Got you, my lad!' cried the thief, breathless but triumphant. 'Thought you could outsmart me, eh? I'll give you "stupid Sassynack".'

'You leave me alone!' cried Robbie in a terrified voice. 'I'll get my dad on to you.'

'Fortunately,' said Tyler, almost to himself, 'your dad ain't around at the moment. Come on, Robbie boy, shall I pull you and dangle you, or are you goin' to come nice and easy?'

Robbie tried to kick out, but Tyler held on to his ankle with tenacity. There was not a lot of room for movement in the chimney and soon Robbie was sobbing with frustration.

'Let me go,' he cried. 'You let me go.'

'You forgot to call me a Sassynack that time,' growled Tyler. 'I ought to just rip you off the rock face and watch you take a nosedive down there into the trees. Like that, wouldya? Like to fly, eh?'

'You – just – leave – me – alone,' came the sobs.

'Can't do that, Robbie boy. Sorry. Now, if I let you go, I want you to follow me down, get it? No tricks now – you just follow me down nice and slow.'

Robbie did as he was told. There was nowhere to run to and Tyler kept him within reaching distance the whole way down. The weather had done what it had been threatening to do now, and the wind began screaming around the spurs and up and down the rock face. By the time the pair of them reached the bottom, the snow was lashing in through the trees.

At first, Tyler could not find his shotgun, but eventually after kicking away the snow he discovered it still wedged between the two rocks. He grabbed Robbie by the scruff of the neck and said, 'Right, you, you know the quickest way back to the school. On you go.'

Robbie began moving forward, against the terrible wind, his shoulders hunched. Tyler followed closely behind, occasionally tapping Robbie with his toe end, to make him go faster. It took them nearly an hour to get to the edge of the village.

By the time they reached the school, both of them were exhausted. They opened the doors and fell inside. McFee was in there, warming his hands in front of the fire. Most of the other children – all those except the four at the farm – were also in the room.

McFee said, 'Ah thought you was a goner, pal. Ah'd given you up long ago.'

'I'm all right,' gasped Tyler, as the warmth thawed through his frozen limbs. 'Don't you worry about me.'

When his circulation began to start moving again, it was very painful, and Tyler began to curse Robbie. He called him some names which made the other children gasp, and others they didn't understand. Finally, when he was through, he said savagely to Robbie, 'Tomorrow morning I'm goin' to teach you a lesson, boy. I'll make you wish you never thought of runnin' away. I'll make you wish you was never born.'

Robbie stared back at him grimly.

That night, Robbie lay in a miserable heap, tied to Tyler's booted foot by a length of rope. He thought about what he had done and the consequences of his action. It had all gone wrong somehow. Tyler and McFee, and Robbie himself, were all meant to be lying on the mountainside, dead.

Robbie Mcleod had one dream. He was passionately fond of Morag Knowehead and his fantasies were of her as a Scottish princess, and of himself as Rob Roy McGregor, rescuing her from the Campbells or the English. He was jealous of Alistair Burns, who was cleverer than Robbie at school, but wisely tried not to show it. He was proud of his clan and his tartan, and he was scared stiff of Tyler and McFee.

He had acknowledged this last fear to himself even before he decided to try to lure them into the wilderness. His love of Morag had spurred him into action. When the adults had first gone, Robbie had secretly been pleased. He knew he and Morag would see a lot of each other, without adult interference, and she might come to like him enough to become his proper girlfriend, so that he could tell people they were going together.

Then, when the real effect of the adults' absence had sunk in, she became a sort of compensation factor. His mum and dad were gone, but Morag was there to help him guide the other kids through their ordeal. He could still be the hero for her, but as a partner, a rock for her to lean against.

So it was for love of Morag that he had absconded, and for her he would suffer Tyler's punishment. The reason he had run away was to try to draw the men after him, so that all three of them would perish in the mountains.

Robbie had been willing to die for Morag Knowehead and the others. It seemed that this sacrifice might still have to be made, and all for nothing. Tyler and McFee remained alive and in Canlish Glen, and Robbie might yet be murdered by them.

Chapter Nine

AN UGLY LESSON

Robbie woke, cramped and stiff, still with his hands tied behind his back. Tyler and McFee lay near by, having taken two of the children's mattresses. The kids themselves were scattered around the room, some on their beds, others on the floor. Time was running on quick legs.

A chill went through Robbie as he recalled what Alistair Burns had said, that day in the pine forest.

We have to get the adults back before Hogmanay!

If the legend of the piper was true, the adults were now in the year 1551. On 1 January, 1552, they would be massacred along with their ancestors in the hills around Canlish Glen. Hogmanay was getting ever closer and closer.

Yesterday evening Tyler had snatched the bagpipes from Jenny McDonald and had hidden them somewhere.

'Right, you,' said Tyler, waking up before the cold fire in the grate. 'Time for a lesson for all you kids. McFee, you want to come?'

McFee's lank, black hair hung in strands over his face and behind this greasy curtain his dull eyes became intense. At that moment Robbie saw him as a fiend, waiting to feast on another person's misery.

Robbie suddenly realised that the wraith-like Tyler and McFee were unnatural creatures who not only enjoyed, but fed on the distress of others. It was when the children were feeling at their most scared and wretched that the men's eyes grew brighter. Their faces became less shallow, their gait less shambling, their movements less furtive: they straightened their backs and smiled when observing unhappiness.

He sat up. 'Aye, ah'll come all right. Ah want to see this.'

Tyler removed the length of rope from his boot and then stood up. Next he untied Robbie's hands. Finally, he picked up the sawn-off shotgun and grabbed Robbie by the scruff of the neck.

'Come on then, you lot,' Tyler roared at the rest of the children. 'Get your coats on!'

Robbie saw Morag jump at the sound of Tyler's coarse voice and he wanted to punch the man. Who was Tyler, to bully all the kids in the village? It wasn't right. It just wasn't right. There was little Jenny McDonald cowering in the corner, and Heather Brown and Mary Watson, clinging to one another. And Danny and Sadie staring at Tyler with fear in their eyes. It just wasn't right. But what could a boy of thirteen do against such men? They just had to put up with it.

Tyler sucked at his teeth, the eyes in his wan face like two guttering candle flames in blackened pits of wax. He scratched the bare bits of scalp in the shock of dirty-grey, uneven hair as he waited impatiently for them to get ready. Gradually his body went into a kind of crouch, as if he were preparing to leap forward and tear any slow children to pieces with his claw-like hands.

Only Jimmy Watson had seemed not to worry about the two thugs and he had been so caught up in his own new importance he couldn't see how dangerous these men really were. So Robbie was pleased to see that even Jimmy was looking frightened now. Jimmy had gone pale and his eyes looked feverish.

When the children were all dressed up, they trooped after Tyler and McFee, and were taken down towards the farm.

Alistair and Hamish were feeding the pigs when the group arrived and they looked up, startled to see two grim-faced men with the whole of the village in tow.

'What's happening?' cried Alistair, as he stared into the eyes of the man holding the boy in one hand and the gun in the other. There was a chilling atmosphere about the whole scene which filled Alistair with dread.

Jimmy Watson blurted out, 'They're going to shoot Robbie Mcleod!'

Tyler turned his grizzled face towards Jimmy. 'You shut your mouth. Nobody asked for your opinion on anythin'.'

McFee shouted, 'Tyler's goin' to give you all a lesson in how to behave. See you mind it, or there'll be worse trouble to come. Right, Tyler, let's get it over with.'

Tyler looked around him and his dark eyes rested on the pigsty where Myrtle was snorting and snuffling through her feed.

'Come over 'ere, you,' Tyler snarled at Robbie. 'I'll teach you to run from me, you little squirt. You remember I told you I'd make sure you did as you was told? Well, 'ere it comes.'

Tyler seemed excited. His voice was coming out in a high tone and his face was glowing. He dragged Robbie over to the pigsty. 'Get in there,' said Tyler. 'Go on, over the wall.'

Robbie was shaking with fear now and the tears were streaming down his face.

'You leave me alone,' he said.

Tyler lifted him up and threw him down heavily inside the muddy pen.

Myrtle immediately looked up, grunted loudly, and made a charge at Robbie. The huge sow snorted as she came, legs like short stumps under the swaying belly. Robbie tried to scramble over the wall, but Tyler knocked him back down again.

Then, when Myrtle had almost reached Robbie, Tyler pointed the shotgun and pulled the trigger.

The tremendously loud explosion of the gun, fired into the confined walled sty, made the children's ears ring in their heads. Alistair was not prepared for such a loud boom, which seemed to blow his head inside out. He gasped and staggered backwards, stepping on to another child's toes.

The worst was to come.

The bang was followed by an awful sound of high-pitched squealing, which the kids would hear time and time again in their future nightmares.

Tyler then aimed downwards at the thrashing pig and fired the second barrel. The squealing stopped. Myrtle slumped over sideways on to the hard-mud ground, staining the snow with her blood. The sow's head was peppered with bright spots, where the shot had struck her full in the face as she had charged.

Myrtle gave a few more kicks and then lay still.

Robbie scrambled over the wall, his face a shocking colour of grey mouldy bread.

None of the other children said anything. Little Danny was sobbing loudly. McFee told him to be quiet and he subsided into sniffles, burying his head in Morag's skirts.

Tyler was breathing quickly, his face flushed.

'Let that be a lesson to you,' said Tyler. 'Next time it'll be you, Robbie Mcleod. All right? Understand? This ain't no game. It's serious stuff.'

McFee growled and picked at the scar in his hatchet-shaped nose. 'Ah'm very disappointed,' he said. 'Ah thought it would be some rebellious little brat lying there.' He smiled faintly after this sour remark, and added, 'Who said the gun wouldna shoot very well – if it'll kill a pig, it'll kill a'thing.'

Then, as if he had thought of it for the first time, McFee nodded at the carcass.

'That's gude meat there,' he said. 'Gude bit o'pork.'

Tyler looked around and picked out Hamish from the rest of the children.

'You – you're the farmer's kid, ain't you? Cut some of this pork up for our supper.'

Hamish spoke in his usual slow and even way.

'You have to be a butcher to do that.'

'Garn – you can do it,' snapped Tyler.

'No – I won't,' replied Hamish. 'You killed my father's breeding sow. She's not for eating. I won't do anything with her. I don't know how, anyway.'

Tyler stared at Hamish for a moment and Alistair thought the man was going to strike the boy, but eventually Tyler sneered, 'Can't cut up a bit of meat?' He took out his clasp knife and looked at the pig, then he seemed to change his mind and closed it again.

'Fetch me a big knife – somethin' that'll cut meat. I'll show you how it's done. You,' he pointed to Elsbeth, 'you live here, don't you? Fetch me a big kitchen knife.'

Elsbeth went into the house and came back with a large carving knife. She handed it to Tyler.

Immediately he had handed the shotgun over to McFee, Tyler began to saw away at one of the pig's legs. Blood ran down the knife and soaked the sleeve of his coat, but he didn't seem to care about this.

Though the knife was obviously sharp, Tyler had a great deal of difficulty in cutting through the raw flesh. It took him a long time to get down to the joint, where he hacked and jabbed, trying to sever the sinews and muscles around the bone. Sweat began to drip from his brow and he looked uncomfortably hot. After a while he began to twist and pull the leg, trying to tear it away from the carcass, at the same time uttering a stream of low swear-words. It seemed that Myrtle did not want to let go of her leg and was determined to cling on to it

110

for as long as possible. Tyler, unable to back off now that he had a large audience, grunted and cursed as he chopped away at the carcass, trying to keep his temper under control.

Finally, the last stringy bit of gristle gave way and Tyler wrenched the leg free. It was a messy job, with tendrils of flesh hanging from the bony end of the meat.

'There,' he said, breathlessly, 'nice bit of pork that.'

He was drenched in blood up to his elbows. The snow was covered with blotches of scarlet, where he had been flailing away with the knife. At his feet, the great bloated body of Myrtle looked obscene without its fourth leg.

'Could you get me a wee bit of belly pork, Tyler?' asked McFee. 'Ah'm partial to a bit of belly pork.'

Tyler looked at him for a moment then threw the knife at his companion's feet.

'You get it,' he said. 'I'm happy with this.'

He brandished the leg and went walking off towards the schoolhouse.

McFee stared at the corpse for a few minutes longer, then he tucked the gun in the crook of his arm and followed Tyler.

The children were left staring at Myrtle's remains.

'They didn't need to do that,' said Hamish. 'They didn't need to kill Myrtle like that.'

'I'm sorry,' said Robbie Mcleod. 'It was to punish me they did it.'

'Och, it's no your fault,' said Elsbeth.

'It's not my fault either,' cried Jimmy, standing

111

on the edge of the group. 'I didn't have anything to do with this. It wasn't my idea.'

'You're a traitor, Jimmy Watson,' said Robbie.

'They're adults,' shouted Jimmy defensively. 'We have to do what adults tell us, no matter who they are. That's how the world's run.'

'No, we don't,' replied Morag. 'They're bad – anybody can see that. Our parents wouldn't want us to obey bad people, whether they're adults or no. We have to find a way to get rid of them. Has anybody got a suggestion?'

'Kill them, like they killed Myrtle,' said Hamish, looking down at his father's dead sow.

Alistair said, 'We canna go killing people and well you know it, Hamish – that's just blether. We've got to make them go away somehow. Everybody think about it for a while and we'll have a secret meeting when they're asleep, tonight or tomorrow.' He changed the subject. 'How's Jenny doing with her playing?'

'I was getting on right fine, so I was,' Jenny said. 'Till Tyler took the pipes away.'

Morag nodded. 'She was doing very well.'

'But no piper's tune yet, sis?' he asked of Sadie.

Sadie shook her head. 'Not yet.'

Morag said, 'We're doing the best we can, Alistair.'

'Aye,' he said, feeling less than hopeful, 'well, if we get rid of Tyler and McFee, it might be we'll be throwing away the key, eh, Robbie? Eh, Morag?'

'It canna be helped,' Robbie said emphatically. 'They've got too dangerous.'

Jimmy was looking from Robbie, to Morag, to

Alistair, with a puzzled look on his face.

'What's all this about? What *key*?' he asked.

'You,' said Robbie in a low voice, 'you're a traitor – nobody's going to tell you *anything*.'

'I'll find out – I'll ask Mary – she'll tell me,' muttered Jimmy.

'Mary doesn't know,' replied Robbie with a smug smile.

So the children parted, those living in the farmhouse going to their kitchen and those living in the village proper, returning to the school. Myrtle remained where she had been shot, her body lying in the snow. That evening the foxes tugged away at her, and a wildcat came out of the hills, drawn by the scent of blood to taste her fresh meat.

Morag Knowehead lay in her blankets by the school fire that night. She could hear McFee playing on the piano at The Manse. Earlier he had been playing Scottish love songs. She had heard Robert Burns's 'My Love Is Like a Red Red Rose'. It had brought tears to her eyes, until she remembered whose fingers were caressing the keys, and then it was impossible to repress a shudder. It was both dark and strange to think that this man, who could play such deeply moving music, was also capable of murdering her.

She now knew that both men were capable of killing. Myrtle was just a pig, but Morag had watched the men, not the act, and had been horrified by their eyes: the coldness in one pair, the heat in the other. They were obviously used to such violence: one doing, the other watching. She wondered if they took turns at it, when it was necessary – took turns at witnessing each other taking life from one of God's creatures, man or beast. It made her head spin and her stomach feel sick.

She wished she were a witch and could send them off somewhere by magic.

When she was six or so, Morag's uncle had sent her a postcard from France. It was a picture of a strange-looking hare, with huge back feet and a small head with enormous ears. Morag had, at the time, thought the hare magical, capable of passing spells. She had asked it several times to make things happen, or to put right some injustice.

Then the minister caught her talking to the picture and took it from her, calling it 'an icon of the Devil', and told her to pray to Jesus.

Now she was older she could no longer rely on magic, and prayers were fine but they would not get rid of Tyler and McFee. Tyler and McFee had to be removed by guile and cunning. The show that morning had been disgusting and Morag wished she could have protected the children from Tyler's wicked exhibitionism. He had badly scared some of them. In truth, he had frightened everyone, including Morag!

They had to be sent on their way.

She knew they were greedy men, quick to take anything valuable from the village, whether they could use it or not. Perhaps that was the way – to send them up into the hills on a wild-goose chase and hope they never came back again.

She stared into the fire at the glowing coals. The red embers had given her an idea. There was something in the mountains which might attract two greedy men, if they didn't know too much about the place. Morag had gone looking for that something once, as most of the kids of Canlish Glen did at one time or another in their childhood. She had gone up there at a time when the heather was in bloom and the rushy burns tumbled over the rocks, cascading in bright irregular falls over the peat. She had searched their waters, not looking for sticklebacks or newts as English kids might, but for tiny semi-precious stones. Infants were told they were the eyes of golden eagles, dropped out and fallen from the skies.

Garnets! There were garnets in the streams of the Scottish Highlands, to be had for the picking.

Chapter Ten

JEWELS OF THE HIGHLANDS

'Garnets?' said Tyler. 'They're jewels, ain't they?
Where'd you get 'em? What are you talkin' about?'
He smiled wickedly. 'You brats been opening up a
few graves while your mums and dads ain't been
here?'

Everyone knew it was supposed to be a joke, but
McFee sneered at his comrade. 'We're not all grave
robbers,' he said.

Tyler went red and shouted, 'One incident, that's
all. Just one. And you ain't above it either, see. I
remember you looting corpses on the battlefield,
friend, so we know how fussy you are.'

'That's different,' said McFee. 'Ah didn't dig
them up to get at their valuables.'

'No, but you wasn't above snapping off a finger
or two, was you? To get the gold rings off the
officers. I remember. Cold as hell, freezing, but you
still went round doing the business.'

'S'different, ah'm tellin' you,' cried McFee, 'so
mind your mouth.'

116

Morag heard this exchange with some disgust, but continued to entice the men with her story.

'They're in the streams up in the mountains,' she said. 'Precious stones. The burns are full of them.'

McFee said, 'How come you lot aren't as rich as King Harry then?'

'Well, we do earn a lot of money in the summer,' said Alistair, 'but of course we give it to our parents. They keep the money for us.'

Tyler looked at McFee and laughed. 'We probably got some of that, eh, McFee?'

'Aye, no doubt,' grinned McFee.

Tyler said, 'I'm gettin' bleeding cabin fever in this place. We could go for a walk, eh, up into the hills?'

'You don't believe this drivel they're spoutin',' McFee said, contemptuously.

'Course not, but I fancy getting out in the fresh air for a bit. It'll do us good. I'm going loony here. What d'ya say, McFee? Let's go looking for garnets, eh?'

'It's too cold for us,' said Morag, 'but there's nothing to stop you going up, if you want to.'

McFee sneered at her. 'You must think we was born yesterday, hen. Let's get somethin' straight. If we go up into the mountains, some of you are comin' with us.'

Morag didn't answer this.

'You're right, ah could do with a wee trek into the wilderness, eh, Tyler? Shall we go prospectin'?'

'Why not,' grinned Tyler. 'We'll take her with us . . .' he pointed to Morag, 'and him too.' The finger with its dirty nail turned on Alistair. 'Get your coats on, you two. And if any of you others

117

have got ideas about escaping, or getting up to anythin' we won't approve of, bear this in mind. Your friends here will be taken out and given the same treatment as the pig – understand? So watch yourselves, or else.'

Going with the two men was not quite what Morag had in mind, but she said nothing. There might be an opportunity to lose the men in the mountains.

'Where shall we take them?' asked Alistair in a low whisper, as they sat together to pull on their boots.

'To the Kneb,' whispered Morag. 'There's one or two burns up there that are too fast to have frozen over.'

'Then what?'

'I don't know yet.'

Robbie Mcleod came over to them.

'Be careful,' he said in a low tone. 'Do you want me to come with you?'

'They won't let you,' said Morag. 'You look after the wee 'uns, while we're gone. Keep their spirits up.'

'Good luck,' Robbie said. 'I – I like you a lot, y'ken, Morag Knowehead.'

'I know.' She smiled.

Tyler shouted, 'What are you lot whisperin' about over there – conspirin' against us, eh?'

'We were just talking about the best place for the garnets,' called Morag. 'Robbie thinks the Kneb.'

'Robbie's not my favourite boy at the moment, are you, Robbie?' said Tyler.

Robbie Mcleod moved away from Morag and Alistair.

The first thing the four trekkers did was collect some Canadian snowshoes from Heather Brown's store. Then, kitted out with balaclavas, scarves and other warm clothing, they set off east, into the highlands. Morag led the way with Alistair taking up the rear. The two men plodded on in the middle. One of them carried the sawn-off shotgun and the other had a huge knife stuck in his belt. They were taking no chances.

'Are there any wolves around?' asked Tyler, as they climbed up the snowy slopes.

'Not many,' said Morag. 'There haven't been any in Canlish for quite a while.'

'There's no bloody wolves here,' said McFee. 'She's playing games with you.'

'I dunno,' muttered Tyler, looking around him. 'I saw a stag as big as a house up by the northern ridge.'

'That disna mean there are *wolves*,' said McFee. 'A few deer, aye, but nae wolves.'

A little while later they came upon pawprints in the snow.

'What about this, then, eh?' cried Tyler excitedly.

'Wildcat,' said McFee.

'How would you know?' Tyler said. 'You've lived in a town all your life. What would you know about the highlands, eh? You'll be tellin' me next you were brought up by a crofter.'

'Ah know what's what, man,' cried McFee. 'Ah'm no as ignorant as you think I am. See you, you dinna know your left from your right. If there was wolves here, man, you'd be hearing them, wouldn't you? Have you heard a wolf howling?'

'No,' admitted Tyler, still seemingly reluctant to let the idea go completely.

'Well, there you are, then,' cried McFee. 'What else do you want? You want me to hold your hand?'

Tyler said, 'Funny, ain't you? Well, why'd she say there was wolves here, then?'

'I didn't,' replied Morag sweetly. 'You didn't mention *here*. You just asked if there were any wolves around and I said, "Not many".'

'Yeah, but you also said there hadn't been any in Canlish for a while.'

'That's right, there hasn't – not for quite a while. Not for a very long while,' smiled Morag.

Tyler snarled at her, 'You're too clever for your own good, you. I've a good mind to give you a walloping.'

Morag wisely remained silent after this, forging on ahead through the thick snow, up through the scattered pine trees, to the bare mountainside where there were no pines.

On the lower slopes, where the streams were slowest, the water was frozen solid. But up on the Kneb the children knew of a really fast-flowing burn which would still be in force. It was to this place they took the two men.

Glistening webs hung between cracks in the rock. Frost had settled on the tall monoliths, to glitter on the tongues of granite. Ghostly veils of mist drifted around the peaks of giant tors. All around them the kingdom of whiteness ruled, causing them to blink and strain their eyes against its uniform glare.

The going was hard though, for the Kneb was quite a long way from the village, and the route involved a long climb through several passes, around outcrops, and over ridges. It was not a journey any sensible person would take during the winter. The men grumbled a lot, but Morag kept them going by telling them that they would soon be there, just another ridge, just another narrow pass.

Finally when the Kneb did not materialise, Tyler began to get angry. It was bitterly cold, with the wind freezing their noses and around their eyes, and ice forming in the corners of their mouths. Tyler was sniffling, as if he were getting a cold, and kept wiping his nose on his coat sleeve.

'You leadin' us on a wild-goose chase, or what?' he said. 'I swear I'll wring your necks.'

'No,' Alistair told him. 'It's just that it all looks so different in the winter, when the snow's on the ground. Doesn't it, Morag?'

'We're not doing it on purpose,' cried Morag. 'We *are* nearly there.'

Both children had been praying that there would be falling snow on the upper slopes of the mountain, and their prayers were answered. A cloud was also descending, which would no doubt soon make it impossible to see. All the signs were for bad weather ahead.

They had by now come a long way from the village and were deep into the mountain wilderness which surrounded Canlish Glen. Even in the summer climbers and walkers were lost amongst the rock towers of the Twa Bens. No one had tested their orienteering here in the winter, it was too dangerous.

'Ah don't like the look of this fog,' grumbled McFee. 'It disna look good.'

'If these two don't come up with somethin' soon, we'll turn back,' Tyler answered him.

Fortunately, just after that, the sound of rushing water could be heard. Morag led the way to the burn, which shot out of an underground cavern into the daylight with the force of a high-pressure hose. It hurtled down the steep slopes, over rocks it had kept clear of snow.

'There's a mountaineers' hut above the burn,' Morag told the men, 'just in case someone gets lost or gets caught on one of the mountains by bad weather.'

'What are you tellin' us that for?' snarled Tyler. 'I thought we was up here to get garnets?'

Morag struggled through the snow to the edge of the burn. She took off her mittens and plunged her hands into the freezing stream. The shock and pain made her eyes water, but she tried to ignore it and began searching amongst the stones on the bottom. Very soon she came up with a small dark-red, almost black, piece of material.

'Garnet!' she cried, triumphantly.

Tyler snatched it out of her hand.

He stared at the stone intently.

'I think she's right you know,' he said. 'Just needs some cuttin' and polishin', that's all, McFee. If we could get a bucketful of these before we leave . . .'

Snowflakes were settling on Morag's eyelids as she again searched amongst the smooth, rounded bottom-stones of the crystal burn, her hands numb now. Alistair stood by her side. She knew he was waiting his chance to do what they had come up to do. Lose the men. How that was to be achieved neither of them really knew. They just had to wait and watch for their opportunity. Morag could see that Alistair was cold and miserable, and she, too, felt frozen to the marrow, but they could not give up their plan now. All the children in Canlish Glen, save perhaps Jimmy Watson, were expecting them to return without the ugly presence of Tyler and McFee.

She came up with two more garnets and then Tyler pushed her out of the way.

'Let me get in there,' he said, taking off his gloves.

He plunged his hands into the burn and his expression changed to one of horror.

'Ahhh! Damn, it's cold,' he cried, whipping his hands out again.

'Whut did you expect in winter?' growled McFee. 'A warm tub of water?'

'No, but not that cold,' Tyler grumbled, sucking his fingers. 'She didn't even blink.'

'Maybe she's tougher than you,' laughed McFee. He looked around him at the descending cloud. 'Onyways, ah think we've got to get out of here. This fog's comin' in thick and fast . . .'

'Maybe you're right. We know they're here now. We can come up any time and get them. We'll just have to wait until the better weather starts to come in.'

Tyler put his gloves back on and Morag slowly and deliberately put on her mittens, stalling for time, but eventually McFee shouted at her.

'Come on, get a move on, lassie. Whut the hell are you playing at?'

The four of them began trooping back again, along the same route they had come.

McFee started out in the lead but it soon became evident that he did not know the way. Their earlier footprints had already been obliterated by the falling snow. McFee suddenly stopped in his tracks as they crossed a ridge.

'You walk in front,' said McFee to Morag.

As they were changing places, McFee seemed to slip, and fell sideways with a loud shout. He tumbled from the edge of the ridge, down the steep slope, sliding on his back into a deep gully, to the bottom. He landed with a flurry of snow in a deep drift and sank out of sight. A few moments later his voice came up.

'Hey, ah'm stuck down here.'

'Are you hurt?' yelled Tyler.

'Mah arm,' came the voice. 'Ah'll see if ah can get out again . . .'

'Stupid man,' growled Tyler to himself. 'What the hell happened any . . .'

He never finished his sentence, because Alistair pushed him violently in the back. For a moment Tyler fought to keep his feet from skidding on the icy rocks, then they went from under him and he shot down the same slope which McFee had travelled a few minutes before him. The snow sprayed around him, marking his swift progress down into the gully. He was yelling all the way to the bottom. There was a similar soft landing and then a stream of expletives.

'Come on,' Morag said. 'Let's get out of here, Alistair.'

'What if they climb out?' he asked her. 'They'll follow the tracks we make down the mountain. If they get out soon, there'll be no time for the snow to cover them.'

'We'll climb down the burn,' said Morag determinedly, starting back for the water course. 'That way there'll be no tracks.'

'We'll freeze to death,' gasped Alistair.

'Och, don't be a ninny, laddie,' Morag said with a tight, frozen smile. 'It'll be fine. We'll make it.'

Morag thought about Robbie. He would not have worried about the cold, or the danger. He would have just done what had to be done, without the hindrance of forethought and imagination. That was the difference between her two boys, thought Morag. One was clever and careful, the other brave but less resourceful. She thought it a great pity that they could not be rolled into one – but then perhaps such a perfect boy was not possible?

'It'll be fine,' she repeated.

'If you say so,' muttered Alistair, still sounding none too sure.

He stared down the slope at where the men had gone. They were yelling and screaming at the tops of their voices now, threatening to murder the children, once they caught them.

'*If* you catch us!' shouted Alistair back. Then he ran after Morag, who was already hurrying back along the path, towards the burn.

Chapter Eleven

THE TYRANTS ARE VANQUISHED

Morag and Alistair's journey down the hazardous watercourse was hard. They slipped and slid, they fell and bruised themselves, they became soaking wet and froze, but they were undaunted. They had vanquished the tyrants of Canlish Glen and nothing could dampen their spirits, not even the ice-cold water of a burn in deep winter.

'Here, give me your hand,' said Morag, helping Alistair over a jutting crag.

There was another place where Morag got her coat caught on a dagger of rock, and Alistair managed to release it.

'Thank you,' said Morag.

At one time he would have jeered at her politeness, but not any more. A bond had formed between them, cemented by the day's events.

Down through the ice terraces of the mountain they went; down through a magical dominion of snow, the blinding whiteness of angels; down through the channel of maniacal water that rushed over crags and down into crannies full of the unholy joy of demons bent on mischief. This was their otherworld, the ice kingdom above Canlish Glen, and they knew it well, and treasured its rugged faces, its icy regions. Tyler and McFee might believe it to be a hell on earth, and perhaps they were right, but the village kids understood the crashing mountains, the booming winds, the thunderous hills and treated them with the greatest respect. In this way they survived their passage down the dangerous rocks.

When Morag and Alistair got back to the village, much later on, there was great excitement. They told the others what had happened. The only one who was not pleased to hear the news was Jimmy Watson.

Robbie Mcleod went up to Jimmy Watson with bunched fists.

'Now you've no one to protect you, sissy,' said Robbie, threateningly.

Jimmy did not cower away, as everyone expected him to. Instead he lifted his head and replied defiantly, 'I was only doing what I thought best.'

'Best for Jimmy Watson, or best for the group?' cried Robbie.

'Best for everyone,' answered Jimmy.

Morag stepped in between the two boys and said to Robbie Mcleod, 'Och, leave him alone, Robbie. It's silly to fight amongst ourselves. What we've got to do is make sure the men don't get us if they come back.'

'Morag's right,' said Alistair, 'we can't be sure they won't find their way back. It's probably no likely they will, but you know how lucky they are.'

'I think we should prepare ourselves in case they come back,' Robbie said. 'We'll nail down all the windows in the school and lock the back door. If they do find their way down, then we can barricade ourselves in the school. They won't be able to get at us. Alistair, you and the farm kids can do the same at the farmhouse.'

'What will we eat?' asked Jenny McDonald.

'We'll get in some stores,' said Alistair, 'from Heather's shop. We'll make sure we've got enough provisions to last out the winter. Then we won't have to go out.'

Morag nodded. 'That's a good idea. What do you think, Robbie?'

Robbie was clearly very pleased to be asked his opinion by Morag Knowehead.

'I think you're right,' he confirmed. 'But once the school's ready we've got to look for that pibroch. We've *got* to find it.' He looked significantly, first at Alistair, and then at Morag, whom he had since told about the deadline.

So the children got to work, using hammer and nails from the trading store to fasten the windows. They put more bolts on the doors, so that they could be locked from the inside. Those that were not working on securing the place, carried provisions from the shop to the school and farmhouse. Hamish and Elsbeth Cairns asked what they were to do about the animals.

'I've got an idea for a hiding place. We'll have to sneak out when we can,' said Alistair. 'If they have to go hungry for a few hours we can't do anything about it. We'll just have to choose our time. If the men stay around the farm, we'll have to wait until they fall asleep.'

Hamish grumbled. 'I can't let our animals die. They've got to be fed sometime.'

Once the children had made ready for the siege they began to systematically search through all the houses in the village, for any music they had missed on previous explorations. They found books of folk songs, loose-leaf albums of music, some more His Master's Voice playing records, and even some handwritten songs on scrap paper with pencil-drawn lines.

Angel sang all the written music, but Sadie continued to shake her head in despair. They played the records on the old wind-up gramophone, without any success. Sadie began to get weary, being bombarded with all this music, but she gamely continued to listen. Finally, when the kids had exhausted all the written and recorded music, they once again sat round and hummed, whistled and sang everything they knew, until their lips were chapped and their voices hoarse.

'It's no good,' Sadie sobbed after a while. 'I've let you all down. I canna remember the tune.'

Alistair hugged his sister and said, 'Never mind, Sadie – we'll try again tomorrow, when your mind's a bit fresher.'

Hamish, Elsbeth and Angel went on ahead.

Alistair said goodbye to his sister Sadie.

'Can you just try tonight,' he asked her, 'as you're falling off to sleep? Sometimes it works that, when you're dropping off, you remember things you can't

129

remember when you're trying. Will you do that for me, sis?'

'I'll try,' she whispered, her cheeks streaked where she had been crying. 'I try every day to remember it, but it just won't pop into my head.'

'Och, well, it'll come to you soon, and when it does, give a great big yell and we'll all come running.'

Sadie slipped her hand into Alistair's.

'Is it going to be all right?' she whispered, looking frightened.

He gave her hand a brotherly squeeze. Something he had never done in his life before.

'Aye,' he replied. 'Of course it is. It'll all be all right in the end, you'll see.'

Alistair left the school feeling by no means as confident as he had sounded. However, there was some feeling deep inside him, which told him that nightmares always come to an end at some time.

He walked to the farm through the whiteness. All around him the hills and mountains were secrets beneath the snow. When their real shapes came back and they showed their rocky faces, their heathered heads, Alistair was certain that all would be well again. It *had* to be that way, or the kids of Canlish Glen would be scattered and lost to each other, sent to foster homes or charity establishments, brother separated from sister, friend from friend, love from love.

Alistair stared at the mountains, purple-shouldered in the dying light of the afternoon, and remembered something. He took out his *Scouting for Boys* diary. He flicked through the pages, counting to himself. Christmas had come and gone without their noticing. Then he looked up again.

'It'll be Hogmanay in two days time,' he said grimly to himself. 'We have to find the pibroch before then, or the parents will be caught in the massacre of Canlish Glen.'

Only two others knew of the deadline: Robbie and Morag. The rest of the kids had not put two and two together, and were ignorant of the fact that their parents would be slaughtered on New Year's Day.

The wind whistled in the crags above as he spoke, carrying within its shrill wailing a sound like a skirl from a set of bagpipes. These high notes were followed by a deep rhythmic beat coming from somewhere deep in the surrounding hills. The landscape around him was alive.

'Hogmanay with Mother,' he said hopefully to the mountains, 'that would be something to make a noise about.'

Chapter Twelve

THE SIEGE OF THE SCHOOLHOUSE

Unfortunately for the children, all their efforts did not rid them of the two human predators.

The mountains were not quite ready to swallow up Tyler and McFee. While the men had spent a great deal of the time lost amongst the snows, their instincts led them back down from the peaks, to the lower regions where there had been no fresh snow. There they had wandered around until coming upon their own footprints. Triumphant, they followed the trail back to the glen, where the mountains disgorged them once again, this time with murder in their hearts.

Tyler vowed that at least two of the children were going to suffer pain, and then death, for humiliating him and trying to get rid of him.

'An eye for an eye,' he muttered as he trudged amongst the houses. 'That's fair enough, ain't it?'

'Ah'll go along with that,' said McFee.

When the men arrived back in the centre of the village, they found the schoolhouse barred against them. The children had locked themselves in and piled furniture against the doors. The windows in the building were small and high, making them difficult to reach. They also had metal frames and even if the two men managed to get up to them it would not have been easy to break in. They would need strong tools.

Tyler and McFee were incensed by this setback and threatened the children with all sorts of tortures, if they did not open the doors.

'You've gotta come out some time,' shouted Tyler. 'An' when you do, we'll be waitin'.'

'Go boil your heads,' yelled Robbie, in a moment of rash defiance.

Even the moment after he had said it, Robbie regretted opening his mouth. Tyler was not one to forget an insult.

'I'll remember that, Robbie boy,' growled Tyler through the door. 'You'll be sorry you said that to me. I'll *make* you sorry. You know McFee's got a broken arm, don't you? McFee's not very happy about that. In fact, when he gets hold of the brat responsible, he's goin' to tear that brat's ruddy head off his shoulders and use it for a football . . .'

The threats came thick and fast, frightening the children in the school. Stones were thrown through the high windows, shattering the glass and letting the winter inside. Some heavy instrument was used against the front doors, but it failed to make any impact. The doors had heavy brass studs and massive iron hinges holding together planks almost as thick as railway sleepers. The whole schoolhouse was built of solid Victorian materials – good

Scottish granite and English oak – and it would take a great deal of battering before it allowed entrance to the two men.

The building had once been described by a visitor as 'a grim dour-looking construction, reminiscent of a Siberian prison for mass murderers' and indeed most of the villagers themselves would have agreed that it was not the prettiest of places, but the children inside were suddenly grateful for it now.

'It's like a blasted fortress,' growled McFee, nursing his broken arm.

When the attacks on the schoolhouse proved fruitless, Tyler suddenly remembered the farm. The two men made their way to the farmhouse. When they got there, the place was empty. The men searched the whole premises, looking for the four children, but found only animals.

'They widna leave the livestock,' said McFee. 'They must be about some place.'

'I dunno,' replied Tyler. 'They know we're serious this time. We've scared the livin' daylights out of the brats. My guess is that they're in the school with the others.'

The four children were, in fact, in the cellar below Heather Brown's store, where the liquor was kept. This room had not yet been discovered by the two men and the children knew they were reasonably safe down there. It was dark and musty, but they planned to sneak out at night, to feed the animals and milk the cows. Alistair was certain that the two men would not remain at the farm: it did not have the same creature comforts as The Manse.

Alistair's judgement was correct. McFee and Tyler, exhausted by their wanderings in the mountains, and by their efforts at gaining entrance to the school, decided to rest up for the night. They told the children inside that they were laying siege to the building, and then they went back to The Manse, to their old bedrooms.

Alistair had been standing on the cellar steps while the furore was going on outside the school. He had the trapdoor to the cellar open just a few centimetres, so that he could hear what was going on. If he had heard the shop door open, he would have let the trapdoor down gently. Since the rug had been tacked on top of the trapdoor (an idea of Elsbeth's) they would have remained hidden during any search.

Once the shouting had died and the evening was still, Alistair motioned for the other three to climb the cellar steps and follow him. The four children made their way to the farm in complete silence, treading in footprints which had dented the surface of the snow by the many journeys they themselves, and others, had made to the farmhouse. Angel said it was important they did not leave any fresh trails from the store to their destination.

Once at the farm, the business of milking the cows, feeding the livestock, and collecting the eggs began in earnest. While the other three were at these chores, Elsbeth made some sandwiches in the farmhouse kitchen. She had decided not to cook anything, in case the men smelled the food and came running to catch them.

Hamish went about his duties in his normal

serious manner, making sure Angel and Alistair did things the way his father would have wanted them done.

Hamish loved his father, and ached for recognition of his worth. He knew his dad was going to be aghast at the state the farm had fallen into while he had been gone, but Hamish wanted to soften the blow as much as possible. For a ten-year-old, he had worked miracles. His sister, too, had striven to maintain the farm, but unlike Hamish she dreaded the return of her parent. She guessed that her wee brother would not receive much of the positive attention he so desperately needed, but was more likely to suffer under a storm of ungrateful reproaches, for not being a miniature Mr Cairns in that great man's absence.

After the chores at the farm were done, the children went back to the cellar below the shop. There they settled down for the night. When they woke in the morning, Alistair went to the trapdoor and poked his nose out. Seeing the shop was empty, he crawled out of the cellar and across the floor, to the frosted-over window.

He rubbed a hole in the ice that glazed the pane and stared over at The Manse. There was no activity in that direction. He then went to the back window of the shop, which looked out on to the school. There he saw something which sent chills down his back.

Tyler and McFee were piling wood against the doors of the school. It was obvious to Alistair what the men were doing, but as if to confirm it, he heard McFee shout, 'We're going to set fire to it! We're going to burn you! Open those doors or we'll make roast meat of you!'

As McFee was talking, Alistair saw Tyler stuffing magazines and bits of cardboard amongst the logs and tinder they had piled against the school doors. A match was lit and the paper burned, but despite all the efforts of Tyler, the wood did not stay alight long enough to form a strong blaze. Tyler became angry and began stuffing more paper in the bonfire. Then he suddenly seemed to get an idea and looked up towards the window behind which Alistair was crouched.

Alistair ducked. Had Tyler seen him? His heart was pounding fast as he dashed across the floor and down through the trapdoor hole. He waited with his legs shaking against the cellar steps. Down below him the others still seemed to be sleeping. Then came the sound of the shop door being flung open and heavy boots thumping on the floorboards.

Tyler's voice could be heard saying, 'Lamp oil – where'd they keep the damn lamp oil?' Then there was the sound of things being overturned as Tyler searched the store.

Paraffin! Alistair knew there were cans of paraffin in the room above. It was just a matter of time before Tyler found one of them. Then the robber was going to set fire to the school with it. His sister was inside, so was Morag, and all his other friends. He had to do something.

Alistair heard himself shout, 'Here – I'm over here.'

There was a clatter as Tyler dropped something.

'Who's that?' shouted the man.

Alistair threw open the trapdoor.

'It's me,' Alistair cried. 'It's me you want. I'm the one who pushed you. You don't need to set fire to the school. I'm the one you want.'

Tyler rushed across the room and dragged Alistair out by his hair. He marched him to the door of the shop and then yelled to his partner outside, 'I've got one of 'em.' He shook Alistair roughly. 'Thought you could get the better of us, eh? I'll make you damn sorry you ever took a breath on this earth.' He looked over his shoulder. 'Where've you been hidin' in any case? What's down there?'

'Nothing,' said Alistair sullenly. 'Just some more kids.'

'More of you, eh? Let's see their faces then.'

Tyler went to the cellar just as McFee came to the doorway. Tyler yelled down the hole, 'Come up, you lot. The game's over. Now it's our turn. All of you. Let's see you.'

Elsbeth, Hamish and Angel ascended the cellar steps one by one, looking sleepy-eyed and frightened. When they were all out, McFee said to Alistair, 'You, over here.'

Alistair walked over to McFee and stood in front of him.

McFee punched Alistair twice, knocking him over.

'That's whut you get, sonny, for trying to kill me. It's a gude job ah used my left hand, or ah would've hurt you the worse. My right arm's broke, you'll notice . . .'

They stared at the splinted arm presented to

138

them, while Alistair got to his feet looking shaken. His nose was bleeding and there was a mark on his cheek. His eyes were hard, however, and there were no tears in them.

McFee said, 'Now, laddie, ah think my English friend here wants to have his pound of flesh.'

Tyler, however, had wandered over to the trapdoor again and looked down into the depths. He peered and then called to McFee at that moment, distracting him.

'Hey, McFee, look what we've got here. I can see bottles of somethin' down there,' he cried excitedly.

Tyler disappeared down the steps into the cellar while McFee continued to glare at Alistair, as if trying to decide whether to hit him again or not.

Tyler's excited voice came out of the depths of the cellar.

'Toddy, McFee! Bottles of it. Whisky mostly. Hey-hey, are we goin' to have a time tonight!'

A strange light came into McFee's eyes.

'Whisky? Here?'

'Crates of the stuff,' came back Tyler's delighted-sounding voice. 'You should see it. Here, come and give me a hand.'

'Whut about these brats?'

'Leave 'em for now. They're not going anywhere. If they get into the school with the others, we'll burn the lot together. Come on . . .' there was the sound of something being dragged . . . 'this is heavy. Help me get a couple of crates up the steps. This is good stuff by the look of it. I'll just have a taster.'

The dragging sound stopped, followed by a chink.

'Don't you drink all that stuff!' yelled McFee, making for the cellar steps. 'Keep some for me.'

The children crept out of the store and went over to the school.

Alistair called out to those inside.

'You'd better open up. It's me, Alistair — and Hamish, Elsbeth and Angel. You have to come out.'

'That you, Alistair?' came back Robbie Mcleod's voice.

'Yes — they're setting fire to the school. You have to open up.'

There was the sound of furniture being moved, then bolts being drawn, and finally the kids inside were face to face with those outside.

'They'd have found the paraffin,' explained Angel. 'You'd all have been burned to death.'

'Would they do that?' said Morag.

'I think they would,' Robbie said. 'Where are they now, Alistair?'

It was Hamish who answered. 'Over at the store. They've found the whisky.'

'My father's whisky!' cried Heather Brown.

''Fraid so,' replied Elsbeth.

Even as the children stood there, the sounds of revelry began coming from the store. A bottle was smashed — thrown through one of the shop's windows. It went on all day, the drinking, the shouting, the singing. Not once did the men emerge from the store, even to cook something to eat. They took their breakfast, dinner and tea in liquid form, guzzling from the neck of a bottle. By the evening, the men were extremely drunk and still singing hoarsely at the tops of their voices.

'Come an' have a wee dram,' shouted McFee, staggering out of the store. 'Hey, brats, all is forgiven. Come an' have a wee drink wi' McFee.'

The children cowered in the schoolhouse, waiting for a morning which they knew would be terrible. They were lying on their mattresses, anticipating the retribution which would be handed out to them once the drinking was over. Sober, the men were dangerous. Drunk, they were deadly.

McFee staggered over to The Manse, laughing, stumbling over some object in his way. A short while later the children heard him playing the piano: a variety of music from English folk songs to traditional Scottish country airs. Tyler went over and tried to join in, singing, but he couldn't hold the tunes and fell to silence after a while.

'I can't understand,' said Morag, 'how such nice music can come out of such a horrible man?'

Alistair replied, 'He didn't *write* the tunes.'

'But he plays so well.'

'It's still somebody else's music,' insisted Alistair.

'God created the mountains,' said Angel. 'Just because people learn how to climb them, doesn't mean they're good people.'

'I don't think that's the same thing,' Morag argued. 'I still find it hard to understand.'

The melodies on the piano became mournful as McFee got more maudlin with the drink. He swept away the jaunty tunes and gradually sank into dirges, which floated heavily over to the schoolhouse, full of melancholy. The notes were deep and sombre, the cadence slow and lugubrious. Finally, he entered an ancient lament which had the very Scottish mountains trembling at the roots with its deep, funereal notes.

'Minor key,' whispered Angel MacPhearson.

The player then suddenly changed tempo, ever so slightly, and another ancient elegy came forth.

Sadie Burns gave a little cry and suddenly sat up and stared straight ahead, her eyes opening wider and wider, as if she had a pain which was growing fiercer by the minute.

Alistair looked at his sister a little alarmed.

'What is it?' he cried. 'Sadie, what's the matter?'

Her eyes were very bright. Her lips had formed into a twisted smile. Her hands were clasped together as if in prayer.

'What is it?' cried Alistair. 'Are you having a fit, Sadie?'

'The tune!' she whispered. 'The tune that was in the pibroch. That's it. *McFee's playing the piper's song.*'

Chapter Thirteen

JENNY McDONALD, PIPER

While the men were still busy drinking, the children began to remove the furniture which they had piled in front of the schoolroom doors. Once they were out in the snow, they went to The Manse, to search for the bagpipes. They began a systematic search of Angel MacPhearson's home, because Tyler and McFee had turned it into a rubbish tip, and nothing was where Angel remembered it being left.

Finally, Jimmy Watson found the bagpipes, stuffed under the bed Tyler had been using. It was evident that he had been attempting to play them and had pulled the chanter and the drone pipes from their sockets in the bag.

'I'll fix it,' said Jimmy.

Robbie Mcleod gave him a hard look.

'How do we know you won't break it for good, eh?'

'Och,' Jimmy said, 'I'm not like that now. I want my mother and father back again, just the same as everyone else. Anyway, who found the pipes in the first place?'

It was true that Jimmy was good with his hands. He made model aircraft which actually flew. Some glue and wire was found for him, and soon Jimmy had the pipes repaired as good as new. The children did not dare test them though, for fear of bringing Tyler and McFee running to the house.

Once the pipes were in their possession, it was simply a matter of waiting until the dawn. It could only be done at that time of day, with any success, for it was at the waukrife hour when the Phantom Piper came and lured the adults away to that place of oblivion, beyond life, beyond anywhere on the known earth.

All night long, the two thieves drank and sang, fought with each other, and smashed things in their drunkenness. They frequently came out of the store and yelled at the children, saying they were going to make them sorry they ever schemed against them. McFee had found an old claymore, in the basement of the shop, and he waved this weapon in the air.

'Ah'll cut yous all to ribbons,' he cried. 'Ah'll slice you all into wee pieces.'

The children wisely remained silent after these threats.

'With any luck,' murmured Morag Knowehead, 'they'll kill each other before tomorrow.'

'Hogmanay,' said Robbie, looking at her. 'Tomorrow's Hogmanay.'

Alistair nodded grimly. 'Our last chance,' he said.

Just before dawn the children moved out in front of the school. They were all dressed for climbing the crags. Morag slipped an arm through Robbie's, on one side, and Alistair's on the other.

'My two boys,' she said, smiling into each of their faces in turn.

Robbie looked at Alistair, but Alistair gently unhooked Morag's arm from his own. He then went over to Angel MacPhearson and took her gloved hand in his own. Morag raised her eyebrows, but said nothing.

'Will you walk up with me, Angel?' Alistair asked her.

'Och, you'll have them all laughing at us, Alistair Burns,' said Angel shyly, but her eyes showed she was pleased.

'I don't really care,' Alistair said. 'They can laugh all they want.'

As they began walking, Sadie came and slipped her Fair Isle mitten into her brother's free hand.

'You can walk me too,' she said, firmly. 'You're my brother, after all.'

'That's true enough,' replied Alistair, laughing at his little sister. 'And I'm sure you'll not let me forget it for a second.'

Angel joined in his laughter and eventually Sadie looked up at them and smiled.

In the greying light, the children all set off towards the Twa Bens, with Jenny McDonald and her pipes, leading the way. When they were just a few metres outside the village, they heard a yell behind them. Tyler and McFee were stumbling after them, drunk but still able to walk. McFee had one arm in a sling and a bottle in the other. In his belt was the claymore. Tyler was carrying a butcher's knife and another bottle.

'Where are you goin'?' cried Tyler.

Jimmy said, 'It's the anniversary of – of when Bonnie Prince Charlie visited the village. Wee Jenny's going to play the bagpipes on the crags – it's traditional – that's what she's been practising for. Once it's over the Hogmanay celebrations can start.' Jimmy lied very convincingly, and Jimmy was the one the two men trusted.

Tyler snarled, 'You get back here . . .' but McFee interrupted him.

'Leave them alone. Ah want to hear the pipes. Celebration, is it? Hogmanay – ah'd forgotten. Play somethin' bright – a reel, eh? A good Scottish reel, so we can dance in the snow.' And he made a few faltering skipping steps, before laughing and taking another swig of whisky.

'I will,' nodded Jenny.

'Then we'll see who's goin' to be punished as an example to the rest,' Tyler murmured thickly, sticking the butcher's knife in his belt and taking another swig from his bottle. 'I'll teach you lot to leave me on a mountain.'

Little Jenny started off again, struggling through the snow. Angel went with her, helping her. Elsbeth took Danny Mcleod on her shoulders and accompanied them.

The rest of the children stayed on the lower slopes and waited, their hearts thumping in their chests.

Jenny managed to scramble up to the piper's crag, and now stood there with the pipes to her lips, blowing up the bag. But when she tried to play, her fingers were so numbed by the fierce wind, she couldn't make the right notes. It was a difficult enough tune to play in the first place, without having to fight against the cold dawn air. She filled her lungs with air and continued to blow into the bag, her lung power much improved by all her earlier practice. Down below, the two drunken men started jeering.

'Play!' cried Elsbeth. 'Play Jenny!'

Jenny McDonald was a small brave figure against the great stark mountains, her woolly tartan socks pulled up to her knees, her little kilt flapping in the wind, her father's tam-o'-shanter bonnet pulled down over her curls. She puffed into the bag as her fingers went up and down the chanter, finding the right notes.

All her practising had not been for nothing.

Gradually the wailing grew in volume, the pibroch began to emerge, and the glen was full of the stirring music.

It was the music which had once roused the clans against each other and against the English; it was the music which had martialled Scottish regiments against a common enemy; it was the music which had put the fear of death into many a foreign foe.

It was a sturdy sound that came from those pipes – a sound which seemed too strong for the small girl who played her heart out amongst the crags, piping in the grey dawn over the mountains. It chased through the hollows between the crags; competed with the burns that rattled their own music amongst the pebbles; drifted amongst the snows of the higher crags, where the mist dwelt and the sky came down to gently touch the fingertips of the earth.

Jenny played – oh, how rousingly Jenny played! –

as the day began to unfold itself among the mountains. She stirred the very heart of stone with her music. If the trees were not rooted they would have swayed in time to Jenny's tune. As it was, the misty snows tumbled in the hanging valleys above.

Tyler and McFee were silent as Jenny's pibroch drifted out over the glen. They had come forward, to the foot of the slopes, where the other children stood waiting. Tyler was sneering. McFee stood and rocked for a few moments to the music, spilling whisky from his bottle on the snow, but then his face turned to a twisted mask of annoyance.

'A reel!' he shouted. 'That's a *lament* – play a *reel*, damn ye.'

Even as he spoke the sky seemed to grow lighter behind the hills and a frozen passage of air came like a draught from between the mountains. It was as if some unseen door had opened in the heavens, behind which was another day, with a bright, cold light and a more inclement wind blowing. The brilliance was like a stain above their heads, which seemed to spread.

'Damn cold,' muttered Tyler, looking up at the strange light in the sky.

At that moment Alistair heard the sound of the pibroch, far in the distant hills, echoing Jenny's tune.

'Cold as hell,' said McFee, hunching.

Down the slopes from the crag, a heavy mist began to descend in successive waves. It seemed to flow into the glen over the saddle between the Twa Bens, like a broad river softly rolling over its banks and flooding the surrounding countryside. It forced the two men to a halt. They stood still, waiting for it to clear enough for them to see their way back down to the village. It enveloped them, smothering all.

Jenny stopped playing, the mouthpiece dropping from her lips. She stepped off the crag and Angel held her, hugging her. They stood and shivered, trapped by the chill white embracing cloud.

The two men stared at the cloud as it swirled around them. The night's drinking was beginning to tell on them. They looked haggard and worn, the bags under their eyes even darker and heavier. They were both shaking violently with the cold.

'Ah'm freezin',' grumbled McFee, throwing away his empty bottle. 'Ah wish this fog would disappear.'

'It's the drink,' Tyler said, shaking so much his teeth were rattling. 'Brings down the humours of the body. We'll be all right once we get back to the store. I'm goin' to do somethin' about these brats first. They've messed me around once too often.'

Almost as he said these words a howling wind swept down from the high crags and blew the mist into thin patches of vapour which were soon scattered over the glen floor.

'Let's go,' growled Tyler, grabbing Morag roughly. 'Come on you, we ain't got all day.'

'And you,' snarled McFee, getting hold of Alistair. 'You two are finished.'

The two men, with Morag and Alistair between them, staggered back towards the village.

'Didn't work, did it? Tryin' to lose us up in the mountains,' jeered McFee at the children. 'Now we'll see who's boss around here.'

They reached the edge of the Canlish Glen village and were about to drag Morag and Alistair into the store, where more of their precious whisky was waiting for them, when a big burly postman stepped out of a nearby porch.

'What's all this then?' cried the postman. 'What's going on here? Alistair Burns? Morag Knowehead? You two,' he addressed Tyler and McFee, 'what are you doing with those children?'

The two outsiders stopped in their tracks, stunned for a few moments, but they soon recovered. The muscles went slack in Tyler's drawn face, giving him the haggard look of a trapped animal. McFee straightened to his full height though, and thrust his head forward.

'Who asked you to stick your nose in?' he snarled, holding his bottle like a weapon.

'Yeah,' sneered Tyler, recovering from his shock, 'keep your snout to yourself.'

The postman stepped forward with a grim expression on his face and punched Tyler on the jaw, sending the thief flying over the snow and on to his back.

'That's my goddaughter you've got there,' said the postman. 'Keep your hands off her!'

McFee immediately let go of Morag, drew his sword with his good arm and tried to swing it at the postman's head.

'Ah'll have you,' cried McFee. 'Ah'll cut yer damned head off, so ah will.'

Robbie Mcleod waited no longer. He gave out a yell and bought McFee crashing to the ground with a rugby tackle. McFee screamed, having fallen on his broken arm. While he lay winded and in agony, four or five children jumped on him and sat on his head and shoulders.

Tyler was also pounced upon by an equal number of kids, determined to hold him down.

'Get the hell off me!' shouted Tyler.

'Ah'll kill you all!' screamed McFee, kicking out with his legs and flailing with his good arm.

At that moment other adults began to appear from different directions. They swept down on the group of adults and children. The postman quickly informed them that they had two hostile strangers in the village.

'They were bothering the children,' he said.

The two thieves struggled, throwing the kids off their backs, but stronger hands were available to restrain them.

Mr Watson cried, 'Oh were they? We'll see about that,' and pulled Tyler roughly to his feet.

Tyler was interested in physical violence only if he was delivering it.

But McFee was made of sterner stuff.

Despite his injured arm McFee kicked and scratched and punched until he was sobbing with exhaustion. Finally, Mr Mcleod and Mr Cairns bore him to the ground and tied his good arm behind his back with one of the children's scarves.

'Ah'll have you, so ah will!' sobbed McFee. 'Ah'll make yous all sorry . . .'

'Pathetic,' said Morag, as he was dragged away.

The two thieves were locked in a spare storeroom, until it could be decided what to do with them.

Amongst the people of Canlish there was much hugging and kissing, with everyone calling to each other, and Grandmas and Grandpas looking bewildered, and Dads and Mums taking turns to hold their children, and children themselves submitting to being held and getting embarrassed with all the attention.

Once things had calmed down a bit, and wild, uninhibited greetings had been reduced to nods and smiles, the children told their story.

When the adults learned what the two men had done to the village, the houses they had stolen from, the damage they had caused, the men remained locked up. They would be handed over to the police, once the thaw came. Until that time Tyler and McFee were to be prisoners of the people of Canlish Glen.

Chapter Fourteen

THE HOMECOMING

Alistair and Sadie squeezed their mother and showed her they were happy to have her home. She in turn looked radiant and pleased to be back with them. In a way she seemed a little younger than before she went away. Her eyes were brighter and somehow deeper than before. Her movements were quicker, less heavy. Her laugh was clearer and easier.

'What have you been up to, while I was gone?' she asked.

'Looking after ourselves,' said Sadie. 'What were *you* up to in that place you went to?'

Their mother suddenly looked misty-eyed and distant, as if trying to recall a lost memory, but managing only to retrieve just a wisp of it. There was a kind of faraway sadness and deeply ingrained fear in her every time the incident was mentioned after that, but not the kind of solid, dull unhappiness they used to see in her before she went away. This time it was almost as if she enjoyed being melancholy. When Sadie asked her about it, while Alistair was out of the room, her mother said, 'I was thinking about your father.'

Alistair didn't think too much about it, one way or the other. He didn't like to see his mother unhappy in any way, so he learned not to say anything about the Phantom Piper. Alistair knew one thing, that he had missed his mother while she had been gone.

Alistair's sensitive ears never again heard the sounds of pipe, drum and battle noise beneath the wind, as he had done when the adults were in that other place and time. The highlands of *then* had returned to become the highlands of *now*. He stopped to listen occasionally, of course, but when he heard nothing but the dotterel and the ptarmigan, he smiled to himself and went upon his way.

Morag Knowehead's parents were pleased to see their daughter, of course, but since Morag was not one to boast about her achievements they knew very little about the role she had played in keeping the children safe from harm. They did not know that Morag was the one who had suggested and organised the running of the businesses in the absence of the adults. They did not know that she was instrumental in getting Tyler and McFee out of the village and had lost them in the mountains: a brave and dangerous thing to do.

However, Morag had an older sister, of fifteen, who had accompanied the adults. Sarah gradually learned from the other children just how much her sister had done for them. She was greatly impressed.

'I shan't say anything to Mum and Dad,' Sarah told Morag, 'because they wouldn't understand in a million years, but *I* think you're a hero.'

'Och,' said Morag, flushing with pride, 'I just did what I had to do. You might have had to face worse.'

Sarah went misty in the same way that Mrs Burns did when she tried to remember where the piper had taken them.

'I don't know about that. I *feel* something, but I can't properly remember. But you, you're the best of them, Morag Knowehead,' replied her sister with equal pride. 'You're a true Scot, so you are.'

The Mcleod brothers received much praise from their parents for keeping the bakery going.

Robbie was hardly listening to them, however. His mind was on Morag and the promise of long walks in the springtime. He had promised to show her a burn where the trout were in plenty. She had said she would take him to a secret place of hers, a cave shown to her by her grandfather. Robbie Mcleod's head was full of soft thoughts which he would never have dared to share with anyone else in his family.

Hamish and Elsbeth Cairns went home with their mother and father, back to the farmhouse.

Hamish's father said, 'You and I, Hamish, will make a tour of the farm – an inspection, so to speak – and you will explain to me what you did for the welfare of the stock, in my absence.'

It was the moment Hamish had been dreading.

He went round with his father, explaining what he had done and how he had done it. His father listened in silence, his gnarled, weathered hands behind his back. Even when they came across the corpse of Myrtle, still stiff amongst the snow, Farmer Cairns did not interrupt his son's flow.

Lastly Hamish explained about the shotgun, then waited for his father's criticism of his actions.

Farmer Cairns stood a long while staring at the mountains, as if searching for something there.

Finally he turned to his son, and said quietly, 'You did right fine, Hamish, and I'm very proud of you.'

'I did?' cried Hamish surprised.

His father looked at him sadly. 'How old are you, son?'

'Ten, Father, you know that.'

'Ten years old. You know I wouldn't have been able to do half the things you've done, when I was ten. My expectations of you have always been high — perhaps much too high — and here you have exceeded them. If ever you think I'm being too hard on you in the future, you must kick me on the shins.'

It was the first joke his father had ever made, so far as Hamish knew.

Hamish's eyes widened. 'Och, I couldna do that, Father.'

'And why not, may I ask?'

'Because — because you're my father.'

'Then I should know better, shouldn't I? Now, away and play somewhere. I want a few words with your sister too. It won't hurt me to get all my sins off my chest in one day. I've not been that easy on her either, but she's a bit more spongy than you, Hamish. She can soak it up and squeeze it out when I'm not there. I'll speak to her now, I think.'

Farmer Cairns stared at his dead pig. 'Poor old Myrtle – she gave me a few farrows, that one. There she lies, three-legged and nae life in her. Slaughtered by men who are lower than animals themselves. It's a sad end for a good breeding sow.'

Hamish left his father musing over the corpse and went to tell Elsbeth she was to go and see him at the pen.

'What for?' asked Elsbeth.

'Och, he just wants to tell you he's fond of you, I suppose,' said Hamish, 'and it's no use raising your brows at me like that. It's no my idea.' He paused for a moment, then added, 'I wonder where the grown-ups have been? They must have said somethin' to Dad in that place. You go and see. Very strange.'

Similar sorts of things were happening to children all over the village. The Watsons were extremely proud of the fact that their children had kept the school going. Angel MacPhearson's father, the minister, was quietly pleased with his daughter for helping to see to the spiritual needs of his flock in his absence, as well as working on the farm. 'Body and soul,' he said in satisfaction. 'Ye kept them baith well tended, daughter.' Heather Brown was praised for her work behind the counter of the stores. Jenny McDonald was stopped in the street by adults for months afterwards and lauded for her piping: it was she, after all, who had brought them all back from that mysterious place about which even they could not speak.

The children were glad it was all over, but they were happy with the changes. Besides all this, there was great excitement in the air.

The adults had made it home for Hogmanay.

On New Year's Day, early in the morning, Tyler and McFee escaped from the storeroom.

Laughing, they ran from the village, following the footprints left by the adults when they had returned from amongst the crags. Their pockets were stuffed full of trinkets and tobacco. Tyler still had his soft leather pouch, which held the bits and pieces robbed from corpses. McFee was weighted down with coins, sewn into the lining of his greatcoat.

'We'll soon be out of here,' said McFee, hunching into his thick greatcoat. 'They canna stop us now. All we have to do is follow these footprints up and over the mountains.'

'Yeah,' Tyler said, 'they must have come over from the outside, eh? Where else would they have come from? I mean, this path has got to lead *somewhere*? We got to stick *exactly* to these prints they made.'

Before they went high up into the mists, Tyler stopped and turned, gesturing at the village, stark in the clear morning air.

'Good riddance,' he said.

'Aye,' cried McFee, 'good riddance to bad rubbish.'

It was then that they heard the martial sound of

bagpipes, coming from beyond the ridge ahead of them.

'Sounds like someone's still celebrating Hogmanay over that hill,' said Tyler. 'I think we can help them enjoy themselves.'

He took out his clasp knife and flicked it open.

McFee did the same.

The pair laughed again and then followed the trail of footprints which wound into the shrouded crags. If they had bothered to look back again, just once more as they were walking, they might have seen the village of Canlish Glen vanishing, as if falling away into another time.

But they were too intent on the trail before them, and the lure of the music, to worry about what was going on behind. By the time they realised something was wrong — when they saw the fierce Highlanders charging up the slopes, wielding their swords and screaming their harsh battle-cry — it was far, far too late.

Tyler and McFee were never seen or heard of again.